CHANCE FORTUNE
and the
Outlaws

CHANCE FORTUNE

and the Outlaws

SHANE BERRYHILL

Clifton Park - Halfmoon Public Library

STARSCAPE

A Tom Doherty Associates Book   New York

475 Moe Road

Clifton Park, New York 12065

CHANCE FORTUNE AND THE OUTLAWS

Copyright © 2006 by Shane Berryhill

This book is printed on acid-free paper.

A Starscape Book
Published by Tom Doherty Associates, LLC
175 Fifth Avenue
New York, NY 10010

www.tor.com

Library of Congress Cataloging-in-Publication Data

Berryhill, Shane.
Chance Fortune and the Outlaws / Shane Berryhill. — 1st ed.
p. cm.
"A Tom Doherty Associates Book."
ISBN-13: 978-0-765-31468-0
ISBN-10: 0-765-31468-1 (alk. paper)
I. Title.
PS3602.E768C47   2006
813'.6—dc22
2005036400

First Edition: August 2006

Printed in the United States of America

0 9 8 7 6 5 4 3 2 1

For my family and friends, past, present, and future.
I love you all.

A glorious place, a glorious age, I tell you! A very Neon Renaissance—and the myths that actually touched you at that time—not Hercules, Orpheus, Ulysses, and Aeneas—but Superman, Captain Marvel, Batman.

—TOM WOLFE,
The Electric Kool-Aid Acid Test

ooo

Luck is what happens when preparation meets opportunity.

—SENECA,
ROMAN DRAMATIST, PHILOSOPHER, AND POLITICIAN

ooo

Never, never, never give up!

—SIR WINSTON CHURCHILL

CHANCE FORTUNE
and the
Outlaws

Prologue

Joshua Brent Blevins had wanted to be a superhero for as long as he could remember. The only problem was he didn't have any superpowers. But Josh wasn't about to let that stop him.

It was a humid summer day in the early twenty-first century—on an Earth much like our own—that nine-year-old Josh Blevins and his friend Eddie Gardner, also age nine, stood outside the yard belonging to Littleton, Tennessee's newest resident.

"You go knock," Josh said, pointing to the front door of the old two-story brick house.

"Me?" Eddie asked. "You're the one who wanted to come here. You go knock!"

"Let's go do it together," Josh said.

"I don't know, Josh," Eddie said. "Jimmie Donnelly said he saw them bring a coffin in there!"

"Jimmie don't know nothing! My mom said it was a sarcophagus, like those they buried the pharaohs in—something this guy probably picked up during his travels. And besides, he ain't no spook. He's not that kind. He's—he's—well, just look!"

Josh reached into his back pocket and pulled out a rolled-up comic book for Eddie to see. This comic wasn't like any Eddie had ever seen before. It was very old, its pulpy edges in tatters. Eddie unrolled it and flipped through the pages. They were poorly illustrated compared to the cover's near-photographic painting. Eddie closed the funny book and looked at the cover once more. Across the top in big, bold cursive script it read,

The Adventurers

Beneath the funny book's title, the cover showed a handsome blond man in a mask, cape, and pants that bulged out at the thighs. The man in the painting held a beautiful young woman at his side. They swung across a lake filled with fierce alligators snapping at them with long, terrible jaws.

"What kind of pants are those?" Eddie asked.

"Jodhpurs," Josh said as if that explained everything.

"Oh," Eddie said. "That's cool. But so what?"

Josh snatched the funny book out of Eddie's hand, glaring at him as if he were the most ignorant person in the world. He stabbed at the cover with his index finger.

"So," Josh said, "I think that's him!"

"What? Jimmie said the guy who moved in here looks like he's a hundred years old!"

"Not him now, Eddie! But when he was younger."

"That's silly, Josh. What would someone like that be doing in Littleton?"

"I don't know. Maybe he's incognito."

"In-cog-what?"

"Lying low, so the bad guys can't find him."

"I don't believe that. You're just dreaming again, Josh. You play *superhero* so much you've gotten things mixed up in your head!"

"I have not," Josh said. "It's him, Eddie! It has to be. He's my only chance!"

"Chance for what?" a smooth, regal voice asked.

Josh and Eddie turned in the voice's direction. Looming over them was a tall, silver-haired man. He was old and rested some of his weight on a fancy black cane, but he was still far from the hundred-year-old man described by Jimmie Donnelly.

Josh heard Eddie gasp. He turned and saw his friend sprinting down the street like his head was on fire and his butt was catching.

"Chance for what?" the old man repeated in his upper-class British accent.

Josh opened his mouth to speak and something in no way resembling the eloquent speech he'd practiced for two days came out.

"To be you! Or . . . or . . . to be *like* you. I don't have any superpowers, but I saw you didn't, either. And then you came to town! Out of all the places in the world you showed up in Littleton and I knew it had to be fate, because I want to be a superhero more than anything in the world."

Josh sucked in a huge breath of air.

"I lie awake at night just dreaming about it! And I knew it was you! I could tell! Eddie didn't believe me, but I knew it was. Please teach me! I'll work day and night! Well, not during the day, because I have to go to school, except in the summer, and I have to sleep at night, but I could still come in the morning and after school! I—"

The old man reached down and took the funny book from Josh's hand. Josh held his breath in anticipation. The old man gazed at the funny book. A crooked smile crossed his lips. Then he handed the comic back to Josh.

"I'm sorry, lad, but that was a long time ago. There are rules now. The Academy—"

"They'd take me if you trained me! I'll do whatever you tell me, honest! Please, mister! It's everything I ever wanted."

The old man sighed and shifted his weight on his cane.

"The shaolin monks of Kaochan Village made me wait ten days before admitting me into their temple," the man said. "However, you look aptly determined. And I'm admittedly not getting any younger!

"I'm Fearless," the old man continued, a mischievous smile upon his face. "Captain Charles Fearless. Not *mister*. And how are you called, young sir?"

"Joshua Blevins, sir. Uh, Josh."

The Captain looked Josh up and down, then poked Josh's ample belly with his cane.

"That's quite the paunch you've got there, Master Joshua. Especially for such a young lad as yourself."

Josh gulped in embarrassment.

"Nothing we shan't work off, though."

1

"Bishop to D-Six," Captain Fearless said. "Now, do a handstand and close your eyes."

Josh drew his body into a handstand atop the bench where he'd been sitting. In his upside-down position, Josh's shaggy hair hung from his scalp like a brown mop. Captain Fearless switched the two chess pieces, removing Josh's from the chessboard painted onto the table between them. The Captain waited until Josh had closed his gray eyes and then placed one of his rooks, which Josh had previously captured, back into play. The old man leaned back in his lawn chair, a satisfied grin on his face.

It was over eighty degrees outside, yet not a single bead of sweat could be found on Josh. Earlier in the day, Josh had ventured into his mental fortress—a thought construct he'd built over the years inside his mind to organize his memories and increase his bodily control. That was one of the first things

Captain Fearless had shown him how to do during his five years of training. Chance entered the fortress's boiler room, his mind's representation of his internal thermostat, and turned the boiler's gauges down to a pleasant seventy-two degrees Fahrenheit.

"Now where was I?" Captain Fearless asked. "Oh yes—so there we were, the Don and myself, leaping rooftop to rooftop! The island erupting around us—"

"Bishop to G-One. Bishop takes rook," Josh interrupted. He opened his eyes and reached for his chess piece, balancing himself atop one muscular arm. The Captain's intense physical training had long ago burned away his childhood chubbiness. Josh was now a lean and chiseled teenager; his every muscle a coiled spring, his every tendon a knotted cord.

"No peeking!" the Captain roared. "See the pieces in your mind, Joshua. You know where they are, where they've moved. Now think!"

Joshua closed his eyes. In his mind's eye, he saw the chessboard and its pieces in detail. With his eyes closed, Josh reached out and clasped his bishop. He slid it along the board to the Captain's rook, avoiding the other game pieces, and swapped the two out.

"Our rapiers clashed," the Captain continued, "even as plumes of fire exploded into the air! Then the Wrath drew his forty-fives and all heck broke loose! Sara continued to struggle with her bonds as the crane lowered her inch by inch toward the bubbling molten lava. Pawn to E-Five. Repeat everything I have said, verbatim."

"Care for an omelet, Josh?" Josh said.

"Since the game began, Master Blevins, not since you came over this morning. Insolent whelp!"

Josh recited their conversation without error.

"Now in Chinese."

"Mandarin or Cantonese?"

"Mandarin will do quite nicely, thank you. Watch your tone."

Josh sighed and once again retreated into his mental fortress, accessing the room that held foreign languages, then the anteroom of Asian dialects, then the small closet containing Mandarin. He opened the closet and the singsong words glided from his mouth.

Josh finished his recital and reverted to English. "Queen to A-One. Queen captures rook. Check!"

"Check—?" The Captain scanned the chessboard in disbelief. "Yes. Well, um—recite the thirteen laws of Atlantean hydrodynamics. In reverse."

"You just want more time to—"

"Balderdash!" Captain Fearless roared. He pressed a button on the head of his cane. It compressed with an audible click. Josh's eyes opened wide in alarm at the sound.

Josh groaned. "I know you hate losing, *but did you have to activate the booby traps?*"

A split second later, he swung his feet down to the ground and executed a series of backflips, dodging the barrage of rubber darts that came hurtling out of their hiding places among the Captain's hedges.

Josh made it to the tall cedar fence at the edge of the yard without a single dart touching him.

"Josh, one," Josh gloated. "Fearless, zero!"

Infuriated, Captain Fearless pressed another button on his cane.

"Uh-oh! That can't be good!" Josh was about to take evasive action when he saw his mother's car pull into the Captain's driveway.

"Josh!" his mother yelled as she exited her car. "It came! It came!"

"It came?" Josh asked, momentarily forgetting the Captain's booby traps. "It really and truly came?" A yell of joy burst from his lips. But it was clipped short as a rubber dart slammed into the back of his head. Josh slumped to the ground, his head spinning.

"Confound it, Joshua Blevins!" the Captain said. "Even the Wrath had more focus than you!"

Smiling, Josh got up and rushed over to his mother.

Joyce Blevins was a tall woman with close-cropped brown hair frosting to gray. Josh thought the two jobs she worked had made her terribly thin. He kissed Joyce on her cheek. She returned the gesture and then handed him the envelope she'd been carrying.

The envelope was eggshell white. Josh's name and address were written on the front in bold, black Old English script. Josh flipped it over and saw the Burlington emblem—a bolt of lightning encased within a circle. The sight of it set Josh's heart racing.

Josh tore the envelope open, his mother and the Captain peering over his shoulders, and unfolded the letter. It read,

Dear Mr. Blevins,

We thank you for your interest in Burlington. Your academic record is very impressive. In his letter of recommendation, Captain Charles Fearless speaks most highly of your accomplishments under his tutelage.

However, we regret to inform you we are unable to approve your application. Burlington Academy is an institution dedicated to the training of young persons with extraordinary powers and abilities. We're afraid that, as a normal human, the Academy has nothing to offer you.

Should anything change in regard to your normalcy, such as your obtaining superpowers by way of lab accident or exposure to unnatural radiation, please feel free to resubmit your application. Until then, best wishes in whatever human endeavors you pursue.

Sincerely,
Xenoman, Ph.D., M.D.
Dean of Students and Member of the Board
Burlington Academy for the Superhuman
Member, The Brotherhood of Heroes

Josh felt the sympathetic hands of his mother on his shoulders. He raised his head in disbelief. This wasn't true. This couldn't be happening. He'd worked and studied the better part of his life, forsaking friends and after-school activities just to get into Burlington.

He thought of all the mornings of getting up at 5:00 A.M.

and running until his tongue practically dragged on the ground while everyone else lay dozing in their beds. All the evenings honing his fighting skills in the Captain's backyard while his classmates played football or basketball. All the weekends spent in study, memorizing formulas and philosophy while all the other kids played virtual reality games or zoned out on holovision. It had all been for nothing. All of it. A waste of time. A waste of his life.

Anger and despair bubbled up within him. He tried to relax, to calm his mind the way the Captain had shown him on countless occasions. But it was no use. He'd sacrificed everything. Everything!

Josh wadded up the letter and threw it to the ground. His mother's hands slid off his shoulders.

"Josh—" his mother pleaded. "Son—"

Josh wasn't through. He stomped the letter again and again. Then he kicked at it. His shoe caught turf and he fell on his face for the second time that evening.

"I've failed!" Josh cried.

Joyce walked over to comfort him. He pushed her away at first, but soon relented, wrapping his arms around her waist, pressing his face into her side. She stroked Josh's hair and rocked him.

"It's all right, son. It's all right. Shhhhhhh."

"No it's not," Josh said, sobbing. "No it's not. I'm a failure."

"Nonsense. You're the best son a mother could ask for. You're going to do great things, Josh. Great things."

"No I'm not. I'm a failure. Just like my father."

Joyce's loving hand became a claw gripping the hair on the back of Josh's head. She jerked it back and leaned over so she looked Josh in the eye. He was so shocked at this he stopped crying.

"Josh, I know how hard you've worked for this. How much this hurts you, son. How much this hurts all of us. But don't you ever, *ever*, call your father a failure. He did the best he could by us. More than you'll probably ever know! But that's not the point. You're not your father—*You're Josh.* That's what matters."

Josh stared up at his mother. He considered her words in silence and then hung his head. "I—I'm sorry, Momma. I didn't mean it."

"I know you didn't, son," Joyce said. "I know you didn't."

"Don't fret, lad," Captain Fearless said. "I've faced tyrants, inhuman monsters, even a sword-wielding angel once. We'll get you into Burlington. They'll rue the day they denied Captain Charles Fearless's apprentice!"

"But why can't I go, too?" Jacob pleaded as he tugged on Josh's pant leg.

Josh looked down at his little brother. Jacob was dressed in his Alpha-Man T-shirt and a towel he'd tied around his neck as a makeshift cape.

"Because someone has to stay behind and protect Momma," Josh said. "I'm counting on you, Jakey—I mean, *Alpha-Boy*."

Jacob's expression changed. His pouting grimace became a

look of single-minded determination. Jacob turned to his mother, his fists on his hips, his chest sticking out with both pride and purpose.

"Don't worry, Momma," he said. "I won't let nothing hurt you!" Jacob thrust his arms out before him and ran circles around his family, Captain Fearless, and the bus stop sign while whistling an imitation of rushing wind.

"Looks like someone else wants into Burlington," the Captain said, chuckling.

"One at a time, Captain," Joyce said. "I hate it enough that you and Josh have to leave the country just to get to speak with a Burlington board member!"

"Indeed," Captain Fearless said. "If the Academy had ever returned our calls, Master Joshua and myself would've been spared this trip!"

They heard the roar of a motor in the distance and looked up to see a Greyhound bus rounding the corner.

Joyce turned her attention to Josh and let out a huge sigh. "Oh, my baby."

"Moooom!" Josh moaned in displeasure.

"Okay, okay, but I can't help it," Joyce said, wiping the tears from her eyes.

"Even if they decide to let me in, I'd still get to come home between now and August. It's not like I'm going away forever or anything."

"Not *if* they take you, Josh. *When* they take you!" Joyce hugged her son. Josh smiled and hugged her back with all his strength.

The bus pulled up to the stop and gave a clipped honk with its horn.

"Time to be going, lad," the Captain said.

"Right." Josh grabbed the suitcases and walked toward the bus. Joyce turned toward the Captain.

"Thank you, Captain. You've always been good to Josh. I know you'll do your best. You know you're family and that we love you, and can't thank you enough."

She threw her arms around the old man's neck and kissed him on his cheek, causing him to blush.

"Don't mention it, lass."

After stowing their suitcases on the bus, Josh returned to his family. "Well, hug me good-bye, Jakey."

"Alpha-Boy!" Jacob insisted.

"Alpha-Boy," Josh said. Jacob threw his arms around his brother's neck, squeezed, and a second later was off *flying* again.

"Say good-bye to the Captain, Jacob," Joyce said.

"'Bye, Captain."

"'Bye, Momma," Josh said, giving his mother one last quick squeeze.

"They're going to take you, son. I just know it."

Josh and the Captain boarded the gleaming metal bus. They climbed the silvery steps within its doorway, nodded to the lanky driver, and made their way down its center aisle, depositing themselves in two seats midway to the bus's rear. Josh was by the window. He looked out and saw his mother waving to him while Jacob ran circles around her legs. Josh waved back as the bus's engine revved up and they pulled out into traffic.

The local nursing home whizzed by, followed by several privately owned shops and sales offices, all buildings of brick and wood. The hardware store ran by, then the old town theater, then the bank, and then Littleton was behind them.

2

"Wow!" Josh said. "Isn't it marvelous?"

Josh looked out the bus window to see Nashville's tube station come into view. Like countless others around the globe, the station rose into the air, a massive horizontal wheel of metal and glass sitting atop a vertical axis.

From the wheel, tunnels of clear alien plastic shot out in every direction like rays from a pinwheel sun. Inside the tunnels, tube trains darted back and forth at supersonic speed. While wondrous, the tube station seemed out of place among the surrounding twentieth-century architecture.

"Yes, quite majestic," Captain Fearless said. "A pity they had to tear down the Titans' coliseum to build it. But that's progress, I suppose. I mean, who wants to watch professional football when you have *epic* superhuman battles on holovision almost every night?"

Josh and Captain Fearless grabbed their suitcases and

entered the tube station's main terminal. Everywhere Josh looked, people bustled about, intent on reaching their trains.

"One P.M. tube train to Megalopolis now boarding." A robot voice echoed throughout the station.

"That's us, lad," the Captain said.

Josh followed the Captain to the docking platform and peered at the waiting train housed inside its clear tube.

"It looks like a giant bullet lying inside a transparent gun barrel," Josh said.

Entering the train, Josh and the Captain made their way beyond the seating section designated for clones, stowed their luggage in the overhead compartments, and took seats by the elliptical-shaped window serving as their portal to the outside world.

Finally, when all the passengers where seated, the same robot voice they'd heard earlier sounded from speakers in the train's interior.

"Attention all passengers. One P.M. tube train to Megalopolis now departing."

Through his window, Josh saw Nashville slide west, much like Littleton had moved east as the bus pulled away from his mother and Jacob.

The robot voice spoke again.

"The one P.M. train to Megalopolis has now departed. Arrival time, three P.M."

"We'll break the sound barrier before we leave the county," the Captain said. "Though you'll never know it in here."

Josh looked out his window. True to the Captain's words,

Nashville was already a distant memory. Blurred woodland now sped by his field of vision, yet every one of his senses told him they were at a dead standstill.

"Amazing," Josh said. "Simply amazing."

It was a couple of hours to Burlington. Too excited to sleep, Josh pulled out the paperback he'd been carrying in his back pocket, *Great Expectations* by Charles Dickens, and began to read.

"Wake up, lad," the Captain said. "You don't want to miss this."

Josh rubbed his eyes and stretched in his seat. As the fog cleared from his head, Josh remembered he and the Captain were rocketing through a hollow plastic tube at supersonic speeds on their way to Burlington Academy to plead his case before at least one member of its esteemed board.

"Go on," the Captain said. "Take a gander, as you Tennesseans say." Josh didn't think he'd ever heard anyone use the word *gander* in his entire life, but he looked out the oval window anyway. The Atlantic Ocean now stretched out before him as far as his eyes could see.

"So?" Josh asked. "I've seen the ocean before. What's the big—?"

He gasped. They were headed straight for a colossal golden man who held the world atop his shoulders!

"A statue of Atlas," the Captain said. "The titan from Greco-Roman mythology, holding the world atop his shoulders.

Megalopolis's version of New York's Lady Liberty. A fitting monument, if a little vain."

Within the blink of an eye they were at the statue. Josh saw its base was an island of concrete and metal.

"Yowzers!" Josh said. "It must be hundreds of feet tall!"

A nanosecond later they were bulleting through the gap between the statue's kneeling legs.

"Look ahead, Joshua," Captain Fearless said. "And see a *true* marvel—Megalopolis—the island city of superhumans; constructed by superhumans."

Josh looked and whistled in amazement. "It's enormous! It looks like something out of a *Star Wars* movie! Those skyscrapers stretch all the way into the clouds!"

"It's in international waters, you know," the Captain said. "Well, to be truthful, I'm sure the mer-folk would argue that point, but as far as humanity is concerned, no country has jurisdiction. And the Department of Superhuman Affairs is none too happy about that, let me tell you!"

"Why?" Josh asked.

Captain Fearless frowned. "I don't guess the world's foremost human paramilitary organization appreciates such a powerful city being outside its reach."

As they neared Megalopolis, Josh saw several aircraft unlike he'd ever seen dock and depart among the buildings. And something, or rather many tiny somethings, swarmed around it all. Josh couldn't make out what they were. It reminded him of bees buzzing around a hive. No, that wasn't right. For the most part, these things seemed to be traveling in uniform patterns, like flocks of tiny birds.

"I must be dreaming!" Josh said.

The tube train dived below the ocean's surface, endless deep blue sea eclipsing his view of Megalopolis. Underwater lights positioned around the tube illuminated their immediate surroundings. Outside the tube, schools of fish, sharks, and— was that a whale?—zipped by.

The train was headed for Megalopolis's synthetic island base, a huge construction of cable, steel, and lights, its stalactite supports diving down into the dark depths below. Josh saw transport tubes like their own entering the island like spokes flowing into a wheel's hub. The moving world of water outside slowed as they neared the island's base. Moments later, they were docked.

"Thank you for riding Tube Transit," the robot voice said. "We hope you enjoyed your trip. Please exit through the front of the cabin."

The Captain got out of his seat and strode toward the exit. Josh grabbed their luggage out of the overhead compartment and followed.

Josh hadn't paid much attention to his fellow passengers when boarding. For the most part, they were a typical, everyday lot, normal even by Littleton standards. Most were checking their digicams and holorecorders. Tourists, Josh thought. But just ahead of the clone seating section, three of his fellow travelers were dressed in elaborate costumes.

"Oh my gosh!" Josh whispered. "Captain! Look! Superhumans!"

"Hmmm," the Captain said. "Yes. But doubtful they're a part of any prominent superhuman team. They're probably small-town avengers or peacekeepers."

"What makes you say that?" Josh asked.

"Come now, Joshua," the Captain said. "Put to use those superior powers of deductive reasoning I spent so much time helping you develop. Answer your own question."

Josh tilted his head, considering.

"Well, I don't recognize them," Josh said. "And if there's one thing I'm familiar with, it's prominent superhumans."

"Yes," the Captain said. "What else?"

"And if they'd been associated with a superhuman group of high status, the tube train would've been their last choice for mode of transport."

"Good lad," the Captain said.

"I didn't notice them when we came on board," Josh said. "They must have changed clothes in transit. Aren't they worried someone will discover their secret identities? I mean, all a supervillain would have to do is check the passenger list to figure out who they really are."

"Not necessarily," Captain Fearless said. "They probably booked the trip using their superhero names.

"I grant you, some superhumans do have secret human identities, but such is no longer commonplace. Today's superhumans adopt their hero name and persona totally, forsaking their past with normal humans, if they've ever had any to begin with.

"It's chalked up as a necessary evil. Saving the world is now a full-time job. Supposedly, the threats facing today's world are much greater than my fellow Adventurers or I had to deal with—though I have a few battle scars that would make me inclined to disagree."

"Since they don't have time for regular jobs," Josh said, "I guess it's a good thing superheroes get all those endorsement deals."

"Most certainly," Captain Fearless said. "It means everything to be accepted into a distinguished superhuman team. That all but guarantees you wealth and status among both the superhuman community and the world at large.

"And if one makes it as far as the Academy Board, the governing body of both Burlington and The Brotherhood of Heroes, they've reached a level of prominence equal to that of a world superpower—possibly the greatest of world superpowers!"

Josh and Captain Fearless exited the train, and then boarded a large steel platform labeled *Lift Plank* along with their fellow passengers.

After a few seconds, the platform rose toward a rectangular opening in the docking bay ceiling. They crossed the opening's threshold and Josh gasped in sheer amazement.

"Well, Toto," the Captain said, "you're not in Kansas anymore!" Josh turned and looked at the Captain, unable to speak. The Captain smiled. "I've been waiting to say that since we left Littleton!" He slapped his knee and erupted into guffaws of laughter.

Josh, Captain Fearless, and their fellow passengers had surfaced within the very heart of Megalopolis. The appearance of the city's residents was unique in every way. There were masks, capes, tights, armor, wings of feather, wings of leather, wings of plastic and steel. Chests blazed with lightning bolts, stylized animals, starbursts, astrological symbols, alphabet letters, and every other emblem imaginable. Megalopolis's citizens were humanoid, alien, animal, and vegetable. They were hook, claw, hand, and tentacle. They were a kaleidoscope of colors, shapes, and sizes unlike anything Josh had ever seen.

Josh looked upward. The same skyscrapers he'd seen from a distance while en route now towered over them like monoliths constructed by some advanced alien race of giants. Numerous flags and banners hung from their ramparts. Josh thought he knew what an ant must feel like when put beside the Empire State Building.

Above them, vehicles more akin to rockets and spaceships than cars moved unaided through the air, the sun gleaming off their metal bodies.

Just when Josh thought he'd reached his mind's total capacity for astonishment, he looked beyond the cars and saw the things he'd noticed from the tube buzzing around the city's upper-most parts. "Holy schnikees! They're flying! Without planes or parachutes! Just people! In the sky! Flying!"

Captain Fearless looked at Josh, who was wide-eyed and beyond himself, and again burst into side-splitting guffaws. A few moments later, the Captain gained some semblance of self-control and put a hand on Josh's shoulder. "Pick your jaw up off the ground, Master Joshua. It's time we were moving on."

3

The next day, Josh and Captain Fearless stood outside Burlington Academy's large administration building looking up at the twenty-foot-tall bronze statue of its founder. Josh read the inscription on its pedestal out loud.

"Lord Edgar Rice Burlington. Founder, Burlington Academy for the Superhuman. Circa 1856. 'God makes us strong so that we may protect the weak.'"

The statue was of a muscular, long-haired man clad only in a loincloth. At his feet stood a majestic bronze lion, its face frozen in a roar. A large metal eagle sat perched upon the man's right shoulder, its wings spread like a halo around the man's head. A little girl in Victorian dress sat cradled in the man's left arm, her head resting upon his chest, one thumb in her mouth.

"God makes us strong so that we may protect the weak," Josh repeated in reverence.

"I met his grandson once, you know," the Captain said, leaning toward Josh. "It is said he tamed Mars almost single-handedly. He was a great fighting man. To that I can certainly attest. But gentle and fair, too. What a true hero should be."

Josh gazed upon the statue a moment longer, then followed the Captain up the vast stone steps leading into the administration building.

Josh and the Captain entered a foyer that was as big as an ancient Catholic cathedral to be greeted by still more marvels of art depicting the fantastic. Paintings and busts of Burlington graduates, revered heroes all, spanned the walls. Josh was ecstatic.

A huge young man in purple tights and a mask sat at the front desk.

"Hello," he said, "I'm Jack Hammer. May I help you?"

"Ah, yes," the Captain said, adopting a tone even more formal than his usual one. "We would like to speak with a member of the board."

Jack Hammer shifted in his seat, muscles rippling beneath his suit.

"Do you have an appointment?" he asked.

"Well, no," the Captain said, "but you see—"

"Then I'm afraid that's quite impossible. As you can understand, the Board Members are very busy people."

"But we've come all the way from Tennessee," Josh said. "Can't you at least holophone one of them and ask if they can see us?"

"Most are out today fighting the Gasparians at Orion's Belt. And I'm quite sure the few who are in have better things to do with their time."

"Now see here!" the Captain roared. "I am Captain Charles Fearless of The Adventurers!"

Jack Hammer crossed his arms over his chest, his muscles rolling like ocean waves, and shook his head.

"And this is my apprentice!" the Captain continued. "And by Jove, we will speak with a member of the Academy Board! We will—!"

The Captain gurgled deep within his throat, clutching his chest with his free hand.

"Captain?" Josh asked, eyeing his mentor. A second later, he collapsed into Josh's arms.

"Captain!" Josh eased the old man down to the marble floor. *This is all my fault. If I hadn't been so set on getting into Burlington this wouldn't be happening!*

Captain Fearless lay there clutching at his chest and gasping for breath.

"Not you, too!" Josh screamed, "Not you, too!"

Captain Fearless stopped wheezing. He winked at Josh, letting his apprentice know he was all right. Then the Captain returned to his theatrics.

Stunned, Josh sat back on his heels. A smile spread over his face. *You clever old man,* he thought. *You silly, lovable, wonderful, clever old man!*

Jack Hammer came out from behind his desk and crouched beside them. "Is he all right?"

Josh forced his face back into an expression of horror, doing some theatrics of his own. "I think he's having a heart attack! You stay with him while I go get help!"

Before Jack Hammer could respond, Josh was off like a shot into the building's interior.

Josh made his way toward the topmost floor, guessing that was where the Board Members' offices would be. *Isn't the top floor where the big shots always are? Somewhere they can look down upon the humble masses?*

Josh exited the stairwell and started down a long hallway. The hallway was decorated with lush carpeting, wallpaper, and still more fabulous works of art. There were seven doors, four on the left side, and three on the right. *The Academy Board has seven members,* Josh thought. *Bingo!*

No alarms or sirens went off. Either no one thought the Academy Board Members—the leaders of the world's foremost superhero team—needed security, or the Captain was still tangling up Jack Hammer. Or maybe ol' Jack might be a little hesitant to sound the alarm and be forced to explain it was a mere boy who'd given him the slip. It didn't really matter. Either suited Josh's purposes.

Josh walked to the closest door and knocked. No answer. On to the next door. He knocked, waited, no answer. He proceeded down the line, trying each door.

What am I going to do? I can't turn back now. This is the only chance I've got. Desperate, Josh tried the knob of the last door at which he'd knocked. It was locked. He proceeded to try each of the doors, moving in reverse of the order he'd followed before. All were locked.

Josh was on the verge of panic. "What am I going to do?" He slapped a hand to his forehead and leaned against the last door. Josh was startled when he felt it give beneath his weight.

"Hello?" Josh said. He slowly pushed the door the rest of the way open. "Anyone in here?"

A viselike hand clamped down on his shoulder and then he was yanked inside the room. The room was utterly dark but for two red, menacing eyes that stared down at him. Josh tried to scream but the sound caught in his throat.

"Who are you?" a deep voice demanded. It was really more growl than voice. "What do you want?"

Icy terror scrambled up the back of Josh's spine. He caught it before it could overtake him, shoving it back into its cell with his mental safeguards. Josh reached up and gripped his captor's wrist, intending to twist himself free of his—or its—hold.

Before Josh knew what had happened he found himself facedown on the floor, a hard knee mashing into his back, his left arm pinned beneath his body, his right pulled up between his shoulder blades.

"Please," Josh said, his voice quivering, "don't—"

"What's this?" his captor asked. It yanked the book Josh had been reading out of his back pocket.

"What's this I've caught?" it asked. "An actual reader of books? And a classic at that. Tell me, boy, have you read

Great Expectations or do you just use it to weigh your pants down?"

"I—I'm reading it," Josh said, with effort.

"Really?" it asked, unconvinced. "Tell me what you've read."

"Well," Josh said, "there's a lot of interesting characters. One's named Pip—"

"Yes," it said. "Pip—get up!"

The knee lifted from his back and the iron clamped around his wrist disappeared. He sucked a deep breath into his lungs and slowly got up. Josh stared at the floor, not wishing to see what horrible monstrosity had him at its mercy. But finally, his curiosity overcame his fear and he dared a glance.

Josh's captor was a huge, man-shaped thing wrapped in a dark cloak. The Dark Thing's head was masked by an executioner's black hood. Josh once again saw the thing's blood red eyes gazing into his soul, and stifled another scream of terror.

"Well, *Pip*," The Dark Thing said. "What brings you to Burlington? *What brings you to me?*"

Even with his mental safeguards, Josh fumbled in terror for an answer.

"Uh, well, uh, you see, sir, I—"

"OUT WITH IT, PIP!"

And out it came.

"I want into the Academy!" Josh screamed, almost scaring himself in the process. He reached into his pocket and took out a copy of his application, presenting it to The Dark Thing. The Dark Thing snatched it from Josh's hand with uncanny speed.

After a few moments, The Dark Thing looked back at Josh, his crimson eyes lasering a hole through him.

"Is this supposed to impress me, Pip?" The Dark Thing asked. "You don't have any superpowers. Burlington doesn't accept normal humans."

"Yes, I know," Josh said. "But I've trained under Captain Fearless of The Adventurers. He's saved the world a hundred times over and he's taught me everything he knows. That's got to count for something."

"The rules are the rules," the Thing said.

"Look, all I'm asking for is a chance!" Josh said. "If you let me in and I can't cut it, then toss me out on my head! I'll go back to Littleton. But at least give me a chance!"

At that moment, Jack Hammer burst in through the door. "I'm sorry, sir. He had an old man with him who faked a heart attack. Trying to save him, I let this boy slip—"

"So," The Dark Thing said. "You were foiled by a sick old man and a boy not even old enough to shave. Unacceptable. Go back downstairs until I obtain a replacement for you. Your employment at Burlington is terminated."

"But, sir," Jack Hammer pleaded, "I start my internship next week. I—"

The Dark Thing's presence became even more ominous. It seemed to swell and fill the room with an air of dread. "Go back downstairs now and await your replacement."

Despite his size and apparent power, Jack Hammer cringed as though he'd been dealt a physical blow. "Yes, sir."

"And take this boy with you."

Josh looked on from some dark, lonely, hopeless abyss as The Dark Thing ripped up his application.

"Go back to Tennessee, Pip," it said. "Go back and find some half-wit inbreed to make little street urchins with. Grow old with her until you're both nothing but false teeth and soiled diapers. There's nothing for you here."

4

Josh didn't notice as they shot away from the gleaming towers of Megalopolis and its giant golden watchman. He didn't notice the hustle and bustle of the tube station. He didn't notice the majestic Appalachian Mountains dividing Nashville from Littleton. Josh was still in his dark, hopeless abyss, the image of The Dark Thing tearing up his application playing over and over in his mind.

Joyce greeted Josh and the Captain at the bus depot. The Captain had holophoned ahead to tell her of their journey's outcome. Joyce met her son with a smile on her lips and cheers of reassurance. Jacob had even forsaken the hand-me-down Alpha-Man T-shirt, his most favorite of possessions, and held up a sign to greet Josh that read, WELCOME HOME BIG BROTHER. Josh gave them both a smile and a hug. The smile was feigned for their benefit.

"Take heart, lad," the Captain said later as they dropped

him off at his house. "Things aren't always as bad as they seem."

Josh humored his old mentor with a smile and got back into his family's very earthbound car to ride home.

Back at the Blevins family home, Josh didn't notice the familiar wooden front porch, or the family photographs decorating the paneled walls of the living room.

"You want me to fix you something to eat, Josh?" Joyce asked.

"No thanks."

Josh didn't notice Jacob's toys strewn upon the stairs leading up to his room. He didn't notice the life-size cardboard stand-up of Alpha-Man—a gift from his father—nor the various posters, pictures, and drawings of countless superhumans wallpapering his bedroom. He dropped his suitcase to the floor and walked over to his bed. There Josh lay down and curled himself into a fetal ball, one arm across his stomach, the other serving as a pillow beneath the side of his head. Lying there, Josh cried himself to sleep.

Josh did not go on his usual 5:00 A.M. run the next morning, nor the next. Nor the one after that. He slept in, not bothering to get out of bed until mid-afternoon. He did not go to see the Captain to train or study. He did not even call his old mentor to say he wouldn't be there.

When he wasn't sleeping, Josh spent the days following his trip to Burlington vegged out on the living room couch, staring at the holovision display or wasting endless hours on

Jacob's VR console. He dressed only in boxers and a T-shirt and wore the same pair for days at time. He didn't bathe or brush his teeth.

But he did eat. Josh raided the kitchen at frequent intervals, yielding to the cravings he'd held at bay for so long.

Several days after Josh had returned home, Joyce sat down on the couch beside him and put her arm around his shoulder. "Josh," she said. "Son, I know this is all still difficult for you. But don't you think it's time you got on with things?"

"Got on with things?" Josh repeated, not bothering to make eye contact. He stared downward, watching his brother as he shot marbles, his mind light-years away.

"You know, get on with life. Jacob's still here. I'm still here. You have your whole future ahead of you, son."

Josh huffed and crossed his arms.

"The Academy wasn't for you, Josh. So what? You're a brilliant young man. You're going to do great things, Josh, Academy or not."

"Right. Time to get on with things."

Josh got up from the couch and made his way to his room, still not giving his mother so much as a glance.

He took a large cardboard box from his closet and put it in the center of the floor. Then he began strip-mining his room. He tore poster after poster of superhumans from his walls. He raked his drawing desk clean of superhuman action figures, sketches, and drawing utensils. He tossed it all into the box.

He cleared shoe box after shoe box of funny books out from

under his bed, pouring them into his makeshift garbage can. After a while he didn't bother with pouring them out at all, but simply threw the boxes in whole. He dispatched costume-clad decoration after decoration until his room was a blank slate. Except for the Alpha-Man stand-up his father had given him long ago.

A gift from one failure to another. Josh eyed it, scowling, then stomped over to the false cardboard hero. He grabbed the stand-up, lifted it from the floor, and then stopped. He slumped to the floor with a sigh, elbows propped on his knees, his face buried in his hands.

The next morning, Joyce was in the kitchen cooking breakfast on her antique stove-top oven. They had an atomic oven, of course, yet Joyce often opted for the old-fashioned way of preparing food. She found a strange, relaxing pleasure in cooking.

"Jacob," Joyce called into the living room, "go upstairs and wake your brother. Tell him breakfast will be ready in five minutes."

No response.

"Now, Jacob," Joyce said.

"But, Moooooom," Jacob said, "I'm playing marbles!"

"Jacob Blevins! Don't make me come in there!"

"Okay, okay." Jacob was back a few moments later. "He's not there."

"What?" Joyce turned to look at Jacob.

At that very moment, Josh entered the kitchen. He wore a

gray T-shirt and shorts. His clothes and shaggy brown hair were drenched in sweat. It was obvious he'd been running.

"Morning, Momma, Jacob," Josh said. He gave Joyce a peck on the cheek and opened the refrigerator by the stove. He reached inside and extracted a carton of orange juice. Not bothering with a glass, he gulped down its contents.

Joyce stared at her son, wide-eyed. "Well, someone's in better spirits this morning."

"Yeah," Josh said. "Well, I figured you're right. Time to get on with things." He walked over to the kitchen table, mussing Jacob's hair in transit, and sat down.

"I've been thinking," Josh said, "and I've decided to go for a spot in the Department of Superhuman Affairs—the DSA. I know they typically recruit for themselves, but if anything, I should already be overqualified. They only take humans, except for negators."

"Negators?" Jacob asked.

"You know, Jakey," Josh said. "Superbeings whose power is to cancel out the powers of other superhumans. Anyway, the point is my humanity will be in my favor for a change. Even more importantly, I'll still get to save lives while dealing with the superhero world I love. I admit, being a *D.S. Agent* would never have been my first choice, but you must accept the hand you're dealt."

"Oh Josh!" Joyce said. "I'm so happy you're yourself again!" She put down her spatula, walked over to Josh, and gave him the biggest hug she could muster.

———

The doorbell to Captain Fearless's home rang.

"I'm coming," the Captain said, "Hold on. I'm not as young as I—"

He opened his front door to find Josh on the other side. Josh peered up at the old man, steel in his eyes.

"You're doing it anyway, aren't you?" Captain Fearless said. It was more a statement of fact than question.

"How did you know?" Josh asked, surprised.

"I know you, Joshua," the Captain said. "That's how I know. I know you. . . . Well, come on in, lad. We most certainly have a lot to talk about. More than you know."

The Captain led Josh back into his study. He sat in his chair, grabbing a bottle of cognac from the adjoining table as he motioned for Josh to sit.

"If it's all right I'd rather stand, thanks."

"Very well." The Captain settled back into his seat and waited for Josh to start talking. Josh turned and looked at the holographic fire.

"Yes, I'm doing it anyway. Flarn the Academy. Flarn the law. Flarn that tall black thing who tore up my application! Being a superhero is what I was born for."

He began pacing up and down the room, gesticulating as he spoke. "I admit I lost hope when that dark thing ripped up my application. But then I thought about you, and all the seemingly hopeless situations you've overcome during your career. You wouldn't have let this stop you and neither will I!"

"And what," the Captain said, cocking an eyebrow, "does your mother have to say about all this?"

"I told Mom I was going to try for the DSA. I couldn't tell her the truth. She wouldn't understand, much less condone what I'm planning. It would break her heart and she would do nothing but worry."

The Captain poured himself a glass of cognac. "And how do you propose to go about this little scheme of yours?"

"I figure I can train with you until graduation. That is, if you'll let me. If I were caught and it ever came out you'd been involved with the coaching of a nonsanctioned do-gooder, well, the DSA would have you just as quick. But you've taught me every trick in the book. The DSA will still be wondering who I am and what I was long after my grandchildren are in the ground."

"Still, Joshua," the Captain said as he reached for his pipe, "real life isn't a comic book. A pair of fake spectacles won't hide you, or what you're doing, from your mother or the other people who know you here in Littleton."

"After graduation, I can move to Chattanooga or Nashville—or New York! I can go old-school—secret identity, the works. Mild-mannered whatever by day, costumed vigilante by night! I'll get a base of operations, maybe an old abandoned warehouse or subway station, somewhere people won't come around nosing into my business. Then I can slowly acquire whatever aids and contacts I need while developing my ultimate battle plan."

Josh turned and faced the Captain.

"I hate to burden you with this, Captain, but even if you don't continue training me, I'm going to go through with it.

To do otherwise would be to tear out my very soul. But I do want your help. Now, and once I'm settled wherever. You have years of knowledge and experience I can't even begin to touch. Please say you'll help me."

"There is nothing further that I can teach you," Captain Fearless said.

"But, Captain," Josh said. "Please, I—"

The Captain reached inside his robe and pulled out a manila envelope. "However, before you make any rash decisions in regard to living a life outside the law, perhaps you should read this."

The old man pitched the envelope at Josh's feet. Josh looked down at it, back up at the Captain, then picked it up. He opened the envelope, slowly unfolded the letter, and read aloud,

BURLINGTON ACADEMY FOR THE SUPERHUMAN

Teaching Tomorrow's Heroes Today Since 1856

"God makes us strong so that we may protect the weak"
—E. R. B.

Chance Fortune
P.O. Box 164
Littleton, TN 37380

Dear Mr. Fortune,

We are pleased to inform you that we have accepted your application to The Burlington Academy for the Superhuman. You have completed the first step of the wondrous lifelong journey that is superherodom. Feel honored to be a part of the long and grand tradition of those who have gone before you.

Your pod will be delivered to your home on the morning of August 15th. You are to report to it for transport with nothing but the clothes you are then wearing at precisely 7:30 A.M.

Congratulations, and the best of luck! (Of course, luck should not be a problem where you are concerned!)

Sincerely,
Xenoman, Ph.D., M.D.
Dean of Students and Member of the Board
Burlington Academy for the Superhuman
Member, The Brotherhood of Heroes

Josh looked back up at the Captain. "So this 'Chance Fortune' got accepted into Burlington and they sent it to the wrong address. So what?"

"Oh," the Captain said, "and here I thought you'd be a bit more excited—*Chance!*"

He watched gleefully as realization hit Josh like a lead cannonball covered with steel and soaked in cement.

"But how did you—I mean, what did you—?"

"I still have a few connections in the superhero world, Josh," the Captain said. "A few falsified documents, including a letter of recommendation from my old running mate, Buck Gordon, a reworking of your records on the worldnet by one of his debtors, and presto! You're Chance Fortune, Superhuman at Large."

"But what will we tell Mom?"

"We'll tell her the Academy reconsidered. Your name change can be chalked up to your new superhero identity. I don't like to abuse her trust in me, but, like you said, there are some things sons and daughters must do that their mothers just simply wouldn't understand. I think you'll agree this qualifies as one of those things."

"But what if I'm recognized?"

"No one at Burlington saw you."

"The Dark Thing did."

"He's a Board Member. They have more important matters to concern themselves with than scrutinizing every student who passes their way. And besides, once there, simply do what most other superhumans already do—wear a mask."

"Well, what's my power?"

"*Luck,* Josh, that's your power. Unnaturally good luck. It has certainly served you thus far, I believe."

The Captain and Josh stared at each other, wide smiles spreading across each of their faces.

"I'm going to Burlington!" Josh yelled. *"Woo-hoo! I'm going to Burlington!"*

The doorbell rang at the Blevins household on the fifteenth of August at precisely 7:10 A.M. Josh, his mother, his brother, and the Captain sat in the living room, their bellies full of bacon, eggs, and homemade biscuits.

Josh was at the door before the *dong* of the *ding-dong* could sound. He opened it to see a man in a purple shirt, black shorts, and cap with an e-board. Behind him a rectangular box large enough to house a refrigerator floated a few inches above the ground.

"Delivery for Chance Fortune," the man said.

"Uh, that's me," Josh—*Chance*—said, having to think for a moment before answering to his new name.

"Sign here please," the man said.

Chance took the e-board. Holding his breath, he pressed his right thumb to its reader. In less than a second, the message *DNA signature confirmed* appeared on the screen above his thumb. Chance sighed in relief.

Captain Fearless's friend must have known what he was doing when he reworked my electronic dossier. Chance handed the man back his e-board. The man checked the message and nodded at Chance.

"Put this wherever you can store it for an extended duration, and then press the red button." He gestured to a large red button poking out from the box's exterior midway down its side. Chance thanked the man and pulled the large box inside. It floated weightlessly over the threshold into the house.

Everyone followed Chance as he pushed his mysterious package upstairs and into his bedroom. He placed it in the room's farthest corner. Once everyone was inside, Chance pushed the red button and stepped back.

The box folded in on itself over and over, getting smaller and smaller until it was undetectable to the human eye. In its place stood a seven-foot-tall glass tube, gray metal capping its top and serving as its base. Four flat beams of the metal ran down its glass sides. Various antennae and receiving dishes were mounted at its top. They rotated and waved like the feelers of a living insect.

The pod lowered itself until it came to rest on the floor.

"Well, I guess this is good-bye for a while," Chance said.

Tears leaked from Joyce's eyes as she hugged her son. "Don't you want to take anything? I could at least pack you a lunch real quick."

"The letter said just the clothes on my back, Mom," Chance said.

Joyce nodded in understanding as new tears swelled in her eyes.

Chance turned to the Captain.

"What can I say? How can I ever repay—?"

"Your friendship has been more than enough payment, Joshua," the Captain said. "I should be thanking you for giving an old man a little joy in his golden years. It's a hard life you've chosen, lad, but a glorious one. Joshua—*Chance*—you're the best I've ever seen. Far better than I was at your age. I know you'll make us all proud."

Then Captain Fearless's demeanor formalized the way it always did when he spoke on matters of importance.

"Chance, these last years, I've trained you the best that I know how. But if you remember nothing else that I've taught you, remember this. You have two things that will see you successful in all that you do in life—this . . ." The Captain poked Chance in the forehead. "And even more importantly—*this*." The Captain moved his finger to touch Chance's chest. "And no matter what happens, no matter how bad things may get . . ."

"Never, never, never give up!" Chance finished.

They exchanged a hug and then the Captain made way for Jacob to say his good-byes.

"J— Chance," Jacob said.

"Yeah, Jakey."

"I want you to have these!"

He fished five marbles from his pocket and held them out toward his brother as if they were the greatest treasure in the world.

"Uh," Chance said, taking the five polished marbles from his brother's hand, "thanks, Jakey."

"They're my lucky marbles," Jacob said, beaming with pride. "I've never lost with them. They'll bring you good luck!"

Chance bent down and hugged his brother. "Thanks, little brother. I love you."

"I love you, too, Chance," Jacob said. They released each other and then Jacob joined Joyce and the Captain.

Behind him, Chance heard an electric crackle as the portion of the glass tube facing them disappeared, leaving empty air between the two forward metal beams. He looked up at his clock's holographic readout. It read 7:29 A.M.

Chance waved at his family, took a deep breath, and stepped into the pod. Then he disappeared in a blast of white light.

"Holy schnikees!" Jacob said.

"Jacob Blevins!" Joyce reprimanded.

The Captain turned to face his ex-pupil's younger brother, looking him up and down appraisingly. He shifted his weight to lean on his cane and smiled down at Jacob.

"That's quite a mouth you've got there, lad. Nothing we shan't work off, though."

5

As the clock readout changed to 7:30 A.M., tiny starbursts of white light appeared before Chance's eyes. He looked
up to see his mother, his brother, and the Captain disappearing
beyond the fireworks display. *Well, I guess it's actually me who's
disappearing,* Chance thought as he looked down to see his
body fading. Then his entire field of vision was taken up by
the starbursts.

The teleportation pod's computer mapped Chance's DNA,
translated that data into binary code, then unscrambled his
atoms. He was disintegrated, reduced to unmixed ingredients
and a recipe. The pod broadcasted both Chance's personal ge-
netic code and the atoms composing him via an invisible par-
ticle wave to one of the Academy satellites in orbit over the
Earth.

The satellite broadcasted its information and cargo to the

Academy, where they reformed into the fourteen-year-old boy now known as Chance Fortune.

The white shimmer in front of Chance's eyes dissipated, reducing itself in the exact reverse order of the process that had created it. The solid light mass broke into small light bursts at its edges, whittling away at itself until it was no more. Chance saw his hands and feet become solid again. He palmed his chest, abdomen, and hips, checking to make sure everything survived the trip. He sighed, relieved to find everything intact and in place.

Chance looked about his surroundings. He was in a large circular room with walls of opaque glass. The floor and ceiling were comprised of dull gray metal. Wide red lines criss-crossed their surfaces. As he looked around, several tiny starbursts formed in the air. They weaved themselves into light masses, and more people appeared.

Chance's fellow arrivals wore the same expression of surprise he thought he must have had as the spots had faded from his own eyes. Everywhere he looked, boys and girls his age appeared dressed in clothing every bit as varied as their races, cultures, and species.

"Please step onto a red line and follow it to the building's exit," a synthetic female voice said. The voice repeated itself in several other languages familiar to Chance and also in some that were not. Then the recording restarted its cycle, sounding its message once more in English.

Chance stepped onto the red line closest to him. More tiny light bursts formed over the section of floor where he'd been standing. Within seconds, another figure materialized. It was a small blond boy dressed in a short-sleeve Hawaiian button-up shirt.

"Hi," Chance said, extending his hand. "I'm J— Chance. Chance Fortune."

The boy looked Chance up and down and then seized him by the shoulders.

"Hey, what are you—?" Chance started to say, then stopped.

The boy looked Chance in the eye, his expression neither angry nor upset nor anything at all. He began to sniff him up and down. Chance gazed at the boy in shocked confusion. After a few seconds, the boy released Chance, made a 180-degree turn, and stepped onto a red line, making his way along it toward the exit door.

What the heck was that all about? Chance thought. At a loss, he turned and visually traced his own line's path. It led to a large metal door within the glass wall on the room's other side.

Chance walked the line, making his way toward the exit. He noticed light bursts exploding all around the line, but none appeared upon its path. When he reached the exit, he saw a line of kids in front of him. The door swallowed one superhuman, then another, and then another. Chance's turn came. He walked through, nervous and scared, but excited to face whatever lay beyond.

Chance joined hundreds of his would-be peers outside in a vast courtyard surrounded by buildings that looked like they belonged in a *Jetsons* cartoon. The day was new and still cool. The sun hung low in the eastern sky. The yard was a carpet of lush green grass polka-dotted by life-size marble statues of famous Burlington superhuman alumni. Chance examined a group of statues sculpted so that they wore 1960s fashion. "Wow! Mod Master and the Psychedelic Six!"

The statues surrounded a concrete stage that sat in the center of the lawn. Banners of red, white, and blue hung from the stage. Some read, WELCOME STUDENTS, while others bore the Burlington motto and its lightning bolt emblem. On the stage, seven empty chairs hovered in the air.

Behind the stage, a full symphonic orchestra in formal dress sat patiently, tuning their instruments. Its members plucked at violin strings and tightened drum heads, creating a soft disharmonious lull. Several rows of men and women without instruments sat behind the orchestra.

A chorus? Chance wondered. He was amazed. He'd never seen so many acoustical instruments together at once. His mother had told him stories of seeing such things as a child, but he'd never really believed her. Not until now. Chance's mind boggled at the expense this must have constituted.

He made his way through the crowd to a statue depicting a patriotic American hero. "Cool. The Star-Spangled Man."

"Did you know he was chairman of the Burlington Academy Board during the 1940s?"

Chance turned and saw a short, chubby, chocolate-skinned boy with thick glasses smiling up at him.

"Yeah," Chance said. "I used to watch his old movie serials on holovision all the time. His stunts are as good as anything Hollywood can do today. . . . "

"I'm Percy," the boy said. "Short for Percival, like the knight. I'm from Mars. Everything's so heavy here. Even the air. What's your name?"

"Chance. Pleased to meet you, Percy. I'm from Earth, the States." Chance extended his hand and the boy took it in a weak, fishy grip.

"I'm a *technomancer*," Percy offered. "I can talk to computers and machines and all kinds of electronic gizmos and make them into things. What's your power?"

"Uh, *luck*," Chance said, uncertain at first, then becoming surer of himself. "Unnaturally good luck."

"Doesn't sound like much of a power," Percy said.

"Oh," Chance said, "it's gotten me further than you'd think."

Chance heard mechanized whirring and looked up to see a Megalopolis police droid flying above the crowd. The droid towed a prisoner behind it in a green bubble of energy. Chance and Percy watched as the droid and his prisoner landed among a cluster of boys and girls not far from where they were standing. The other kids spread out to make room, regarding the prisoner with suspicious eyes. The green energy bubble faded away and then the robot did likewise, shooting off into the sky above.

The prisoner was a boy Chance's age. He was clad in a bandanna, leather jacket, and faded blue jeans. His handsome face was darkened by black sunglasses and a crop of whiskers he seemed too young to grow.

The boy rubbed his wrists as though they'd been cuffed, surveying the wary young people around him. Suddenly he snapped at them, leaning forward and biting the air. They recoiled from him with a gasp. Seemingly pleased with their reaction, the boy wandered out from their midst. Beside Chance,

Percy gulped, his eyes tripling in size as the boy walked toward them.

"Got any chewing gum?" the boy asked, his accent pegging him as someone from one of New York's tougher boroughs.

"Afraid not," Chance said.

The boy looked down at Percy. "What about you, pud? Got a stick of spearmint?"

"Uh—" Percy said. "Nope."

"Figures," the boy said. "Well, if I can't bum a piece off you losers, I guess I'll have to borrow from my own stash." He reached inside his leather jacket and produced a mashed pack of gum. "Ah, good ol' American chewing gum. Is there anything sweeter?"

The boy extracted a stick of gum from the pack and held it up to his face. He reached up, grasped his sunglasses, and lifted them from his eyes. Or rather, he lifted them from where his eyes should have been, *for he had no eyes*. Instead, electricity pulsated and danced within the two sockets bookending either side of his nose, threatening to shoot outward at any moment.

And then it did.

Chance and Percy watched as two small bolts of lightning leapt from the boy's eye sockets and incinerated the gum wrapper in a flash of smoke and flame. The gum itself remained unscathed. Chance was impressed by the boy's precision.

The boy put his sunglasses back on and popped the gum in his mouth. "I'm Shockley."

"I'm Chance. Chance Fortune. This is Percy."

"Love the accent, Fortune. Where you from? South, I'll

bet. Regular country-fried hayseed from Hicksville, aren't you?" Shockley eyed Chance, scanning him from head to toe.

Chance looked right back at him, peering straight through Shockley's dark sunglasses into the electric fire that lay beyond, not flinching in the slightest. "I suggest you smile when you talk to me like that."

Shockley's face hardened. The inferno that was his eyes spilled out from the edges of his glasses. Then he relaxed, the sparks receding, and smiled.

"I think I'm going to like you, Hicksville." Shockley held out his hand. Chance took it.

"That was quite an entrance you made."

"Yeah," Shockley said. "The robocops caught me swiping skycars back in Megalopolis. It was the Academy or three years in the pen. So here I am!"

"You're from Megalopolis?" Chance asked. "Way cool!"

"Yeah," Shockley said. "It ain't so bad, sometimes."

Chance was about to drill Shockley with questions about life in the superhuman city when the orchestra came alive with the thunderous pounding of the bass drums.

A synthetic female voice—different from the one Chance had heard in the tube station—spoke. "Welcome, students, to the Burlington Academy for the Superhuman. Thank you for attending today's opening ceremony here in the Courtyard of Heroes."

Everyone clapped.

"Students," the synthetic female voice continued, "please join together in welcoming Dr. Adam Bryson of The Brotherhood of Heroes, Dean of Science, Member of the Board, superscientist, and pilot of the robot Gigantron."

Chance looked up and saw a gigantic gleaming metal man shooting down toward them from the heavens. The enormous robot touched down beside the stage and the band quieted. Gigantron's face opened like an airplane cockpit. A man in a helmet and flight suit sat at what Chance assumed were Gigantron's controls. The man took off his helmet and waved to the crowd. It was Dr. Bryson. Chance knew his face from the virtual reality files of Littleton's public library. He recognized Dr. Bryson's trademark gray-at-the-temples hair.

"The world's biggest egghead!" Shockley popped his gum loudly.

"I think Dr. Bryson's cool," Percy mumbled as he slumped his shoulders. "He's a superscientist, like my parents."

"Nerd alert!" Shocker said.

"I believe," Chance said, "that *egghead* invented the energy-dampening plastic that your sunglasses are made of, Shockley. So maybe you should rethink your definition of *nerd* the next time you're able to look in the mirror without blasting yourself!"

"Okay, okay," Shockley said. "I give."

The orchestra kicked up again with a speedy rhythm of bongos and xylophones.

"Students," the synthetic female voice said, "please join together in welcoming Captain Dynamo of The Brotherhood of Heroes, Dean of Mathematics, Member of the Board, and superspeedster."

A gold-and-blue light trail zipped through the crowd and came to rest on the stage. Everyone gasped. It was as if Captain Dynamo had appeared out of nowhere. He was clothed in blue tights and wore a golden metal helmet with tiny metal wings of the same color on either side.

"Superspeed," Shockley said as he chomped his gum. "Oh, the things I could get away with if I had that power!"

The orchestra played once more. This time Chance recognized the music from the Captain's collection. It was Beethoven's Fifth Symphony.

"Students," the synthetic female voice said, "please join together in welcoming The Imagineer of The Brotherhood of Heroes, Dean of the Arts, and Member of the Board."

The Imagineer rode down from the clouds in a translucent red spaceship so large it cast a shadow over the entire crowd. Chance squinted and saw through the ship's hull that the Board Member was garbed in a crimson lab coat and hardhat. The image of a red lightbulb sat on his chest and a smaller ebony version was on his hat.

The spaceship disappeared and the Imagineer floated down to the stage. Images of red roaring lions and crimson flaming dragons appeared and disappeared all around the Board Member.

"Wow!" Chance said. "To have the ability to conjure your thoughts into reality! Now that's a superpower!"

Then the orchestra began to play a discordant, almost eerie harmony characterized by screeching violins.

"Students," the synthetic female voice said, "please join together in welcoming Xenoman of The Brotherhood of Heroes, Dean of Students, and Member of the Board."

Xenoman appeared upon the stage, ghostlike, the courtyard behind him visible through his green cloak, a high collar framing his gigantic, bald, purple head. His image solidified and a thin, lanky, violet arm sprouted from beneath the cloak. The incredibly long hand and fingers attached to it waved at the students like wisps in the wind.

"Freaky," Shockley said. He blew a small bubble with his gum, let it pop, and then sucked the film back inside his mouth.

"He's an alien, you know," Percy said, "with all sorts of powers."

"What we just saw—teleportation—being the least of them," Chance said.

The orchestra played on. Chance also recognized this piece from his exposure to the Captain's classical collection. It was Wagner's *Ride of the Valkyries*.

"Students," the synthetic female voice said, "please join together in welcoming Steel Valkyrie of The Brotherhood of Heroes, Dean of Athletics, and Member of the Board."

Steel Valkyrie descended from on high atop a giant raven. Shockley's mouth dropped open and his gum fell out. Clad in Viking dress, and carrying a large spear and shield, she was a force of nature, as beautiful and terrible as the approaching night. Atop her head sat a helm of silver, wings of metal spreading forth at either side.

The raven carrying her swooped to the ground. She dismounted, launched herself high into the air, and then came down to land upon the stage.

"She's won more medals at the Intergalactic Olympics than anybody else—ever!" Percy said.

"I could take her," Shockley bragged.

"Ha!" Chance said. "It was Steel Valkyrie who straightened the No-Longer-Leaning Tower of Pisa with her bare hands! She'd snap you like a twig."

The orchestra played, this time the chorus joining in to sing a haunting nonsense litany. The sound was unnerving. It made Chance think of the scary things that had lived under his bed and in his closet when he'd been a young kid.

"Students," the synthetic female voice said with a hint of trepidation, "please join together in welcoming The Boogeyman of The Brotherhood of Heroes, Dean of Psychology, and Member of the Board."

"People say he's a real ghost," Percy whispered. "Or a vampire. Something horribly unnatural."

Chance had heard these rumors about The Boogeyman and more, but no true depiction of him other than those done by DSA sketch artists existed within VR records, and every one of those sketches was different from the next. The Boogeyman was a thing of urban legend, a phantom who scourged the criminal underworld with terrible efficiency. The majority of those who had actually seen him and lived to tell about it were now housed in mental wards across the globe.

Five minutes went by. Then ten. The students shifted on their feet and gazed around nervously. The Board Members looked at one another and shrugged. It appeared The Boogeyman was a no-show. Xenoman turned his head and raised his hand in signal to the orchestra.

The orchestra's trumpets blared, high and proud. Cymbals crashed. Piece by piece, section by section, the remaining orchestra joined them, creating a sound epic in scale.

"Look!" a voice from the crowd said in awe. "Up in the clouds!"

Out of the eastern sky he came, the morning sun blazing at his back. Glorious. Immaculate. Divine.

"Students, please join together in welcoming Alpha-Man," the synthetic female voice said. "Leader of The Brotherhood of Heroes, Dean of Law, and Chairman of the Board."

Alpha-Man floated downward, the sun's rays forming a brilliant corona around his body. Muscles of iron rolled beneath his red bodysuit like shifting tectonic plates as his blue cape fluttered in the wind. Across his chest, a silver bolt of lightning bent once, then twice to form a stylized A—his emblem, the emblem for everything good and right and true.

He was clean-shaven, his square jaw and dimpled chin visible to Chance even across the courtyard. His hair was so black tinges of blue gleamed off it where the sun's light fell. And his eyes were cobalt steel, capable of peering into the darkest regions of space or watching microbes divide. He was the epitome of male perfection.

Chance and the entire crowd watched in wonder as Alpha-Man touched down upon the stage to stand between them and his fellow Board Members. Chance heard young girls begin to sigh and giggle all around him.

Alpha-Man looked back at his peers, nodded, then turned to face the crowd once more. He smiled, and it was a smile that told you everything was going to be all right. It was a smile that said Santa Claus was real, puppies go to heaven, and good guys finish first. Then his face became serious, and he spoke. His voice was deep and full, like the voice of your father.

"God makes us strong so that we may protect the weak," Alpha-Man said. "If you take away nothing else from your time here at Burlington, take away that. The world depends upon each and every one of us. And it does so on a daily basis. We cannot be found lacking. Pledge to yourselves that right here and now, within the reach of your arm, the world will not be corrupt! Pledge to yourselves, within the reach of your arm, that evil will never prosper! Pledge to yourselves, within the reach of your arm, that good will always triumph!"

Alpha-Man placed his powerful fist on his hip and shook his other hand at the sky in defiance.

"That is your calling. That is your duty. That is your reason for being. But you are not alone.

"The Board, faculty, and staff here at Burlington are here to help you see this through. But most of all, you will have one another. Strangers now who will become comrades in arms and the best of friends, shoulders to lean on, ears to listen, backs to shield and be shielded by.

"I congratulate you on your acceptance into Burlington and commend you in your new and most honorable endeavor. Good luck and good learning!"

The orchestra cranked up with Alpha-Man's theme music once more. The crowd roared with applause and cheers. Percy jumped up and down, squealing with enthusiasm. Shockley gave no glib remark. In truth, his chest seemed to swell with newfound purpose. And Chance clapped and yelled with approval, his thoughts only of righting wrongs and doing good in the world. And that was well, for if Chance had known what he was to face at Burlington in the months ahead, he probably would've sprinted back into the teleportation chamber to catch the first transport beam bound for Littleton.

6

After the ceremony, boarding assignments and holo-maps of the campus were distributed among the crowd by up-perclassmen clad in their superhero regalia. At Chance's suggestion, he, Percy, and Shockley swapped dorm assign-ments and in-processing times with other willing freshmen until theirs all matched up.

"So what's the deal?" Shockley asked.

"Well," Chance said, "we're all in Buscema Dormitory, though not in the same room. We go to in-processing at 9:15. That's in about ten minutes."

"What's in-processing?" Percy asked.

"I don't know," Chance said. "I guess we'll find out when we get there. It's across campus at Kirby Coliseum. We better head that way. Coming, Shockley?"

"Against my better judgment," Shockley said, "I guess so."

They made their way out of the courtyard, taking a left at

McFarlane Cafeteria, a large domed building, then passing Waid Hall, the crystalline science building. They passed Lee Old Main, the English building, marveling at its old-fashioned brick and mortar archways, and then reached their destination.

Kirby Coliseum was a vast golden citadel in the form of a perfect cube. Its outer walls were covered with turrets swapping electrical discharges and exhaust valves emitting cloudy streams of bubbling crimson energy.

The boys made their way up to the structure, crowds of other students joining them around its base, just as uncertain of where to enter, unsure if the building even had doors.

"Look here!" Percy said. His hand had disappeared into the building's side, his arm and body now simply an extension of that structure. "You can get through here."

"Wait, Percy," Chance said. But it was too late. Percy disappeared into the coliseum right before his eyes. Chance tried to follow, but was met with solid resistance at the point where Percy had stepped through.

"Over here, Hicksville," Shockley said. His hands dissolved and then resolved as he plunged and then extracted them from the building's surface. He looked at Chance and grinned. "Where angels fear to tread, Hicksville!"

Shockley stepped through and disappeared. Chance again tried to follow, but to no avail. He looked up and down the length of the coliseum's base. All down the line, students were disappearing into its depths. Frustrated, Chance felt along the wall. Solid, solid—then not solid. His hand submerged within the wall, the building rippling like water around his wrist. He felt nothing but open air on the other side.

"Where angels fear to tread," Chance whispered. Then he stepped through into the unknown.

Chance saw he was in a small room. It was a perfect black cube, light emitting from white grid lines dividing the floor, ceiling, and walls into perfect squares.

"Hello, Chance Fortune," the synthetic female voice from the courtyard said. "I am MOTHER, Mechanized Omni-Tasking Higher Education Regulator."

"A supercomputer," Chance said.

"My neural net consists of 563, 537, 676, 848, 478, 478 quantum bits spanning the known globe and beyond. I think the term *supercomputer* hardly qualifies nor quantifies."

"You think?"

"For all intents and purposes, yes. And in greater depth than many of Burlington's students, I might add."

Great, a computer with an attitude. Chance wondered if it could read his mind. Anything was possible here, after all. He hoped the mental safeguards he'd constructed around his mind fortress would be sufficient to keep it or any other unwelcome parties out of his brains.

"I am to assist you with in-processing. In-processing consists of your establishment of a superhero identity, including name, costume, and equipment if applicable. While this identity is totally up to your discretion, the Academy encourages you to consider suggestions made by myself, which are based on your electronic dossier and current superhero standards. This portion of your admittance into Burlington is especially important as your identity will remain set during your stay here once this session is over."

"Uh, okay, I guess," Chance said.

"Have you considered a superhero name?"

"Yeah! How about Longshot? That's perfect, don't you think?"

"I am in agreement. Unfortunately, that name is already taken."

"Hmmm," Chance said, reconsidering. "Well, my name is pretty self-explanatory in regard to my power. Why not just leave it as is?"

"Processing. For your remaining tenure at Burlington you will be referred to as Chance Fortune. Have you considered a superhero costume?"

"Yeah," Chance said. "How about a cape and tights!"

"Such articles of clothing are usually reserved for demigod-level students. I suggest you try something more suited to your status level."

"Demigod?" Chance asked. "You mean some of the students here are the children of gods?"

"Affirmative," MOTHER said, "but that is not a necessary requirement for demigod status here at Burlington. The Academy uses the word as a general term for the purposes of student classification. It is typically assigned to students with high levels of power, such as being able to lift sixty or more tons in earth-type gravity."

"Sixty or more tons!" Chance said. "Sheesh!"

"The majority of Burlington Students," MOTHER said, "those who typically have only one specific and lower-level power, fall into the category beneath demigod. This class is called *mighty mortal,* or *mortal,* as shortened by the students. Once again, this is a general term."

"So I'm considered a mortal, then."

"Negative," MOTHER said. "You fall into the lowest category of students here at Burlington—those of meager power simply referred to as *adventurer*."

"Gee," Chance said. "Thanks for breaking the news so gently!"

"You are welcome," MOTHER said, not picking up on Chance's sarcasm. "Have you reached a decision regarding your costume?"

"Uh, well, yeah. I'd at least like to see what the cape and tights would look like."

"Very well. Please undress and stand in the room's center."

Chance did so, a little self-consciously. A mirror appeared in front of him floating in the air.

"Processing. A costume meeting your specifications will now be constructed on your person using the latest in nanotechnology."

Chance looked around the room, expecting to see tiny nanite machines swarming toward him. However, the nanites were too small to be seen with the naked eye. Black leather boots climbed up Chance's shins and then turned into silver tights, which rode upward to his groin. There, they changed into black shorts, which, much to Chance's dismay, he found to be two sizes too small. He gasped with discomfort, then reached down and tried to stretch them. The fabric continued its climb up his torso and out over his arms, covering him in silver. Then it reversed its trajectory, spiraling downward into a black cape that hung from his shoulders.

"Is that satisfactory?"

"It's—" Chance gasped, his voice high and squeaky, "it's a little tight in the crotch!"

The shorts receded, revealing the silver leggings beneath them. Chance grunted with relief. He wondered if MOTHER hadn't made the shorts too tight out of revenge for ignoring her suggestion.

Chance turned this way and that, looking himself up and down in the mirror. He'd always thought wearing a cape would be cool. But standing there now he just felt, well, *silly*.

"I guess you were right."

"Pardon me?" MOTHER asked.

"Let's nix the cape and tights."

"I am in agreement," MOTHER replied. Chance's outfit dissolved, leaving him in his undershorts.

"How about a mask?" Chance remembered his trip to The Dark Thing's office. "I want a mask."

"Processing. A mask will now be constructed on your person using the latest in nanotechnology."

The tiny machines wove a mask around Chance's eyes. It was basic black.

"Color preference?"

"Black is fine."

"Style preference?"

Chance thought about it a moment.

"I was a big fan of Zorro as a kid. Can you do something like that? You know, make it more swashbuckling?"

"Processing."

The mask enlarged itself, crawling up and over his head and around the side of his face to his ears and then beyond. He felt it tie itself into a knot at the base of his skull and then saw two long, black sash pieces snake themselves out from behind his neck to lie across his right shoulder.

"Is that satisfactory?"

"Perfect. But I need protection. And I need to be able to move on the quick. Do you have anything that can give me both?"

"Titanium Kevlar is flexible while being able to absorb the impact of a forty-five-caliber shell or similar projectile."

"What does it look like?"

"Dr. Bryson was able to manipulate its atomic structure so it appears and wears like leather."

"Sounds great."

"Color preference?"

"Got to go with black."

"Processing. A Titanium Kevlar bodysuit will now be constructed on your person using the latest in VR and nanotechnology."

Tall black leather boots wormed their way up over Chance's shins. They reached almost to his knees and then continued beyond as a black leather bodysuit that molded itself over his body.

"Is that satisfactory?" MOTHER asked.

"Wonderful," Chance said. "But I will need some gear, too."

"Please be more specific."

"Okay," Chance said. "You asked for it! I'll need a grappling gun with titanium cable and hook. A utility belt complete with thermite bombs, smoke bombs, lock picks, multitool, acid pellets, handcuffs, throwing projectiles—let's call those *Chancearangs*—retractable billy club, retracting boomerang with cable attachment, daggers, and any of the other standard-issue gizmos."

"Considering your high level of vulnerability," MOTHER said, "you might want to consider carrying a firearm. Current superhero standards accept and even encourage such accessories."

"Guns are a coward's weapon, MOTHER," Chance said without hesitation. "I will not carry one as part of my day-to-day arsenal."

"Very well. Processing."

A belt of small pouches wound its way over Chance's hips. A holster housing a grappling gun materialized midway down his right thigh.

"Will there be anything else?" MOTHER asked. Chance eyed himself up and down in the mirror. His suit was missing something, but he couldn't quite put his finger on it. Then it came to him.

Of course, he thought, *my emblem.* What to do for a symbol? The image of the C overlapping the F on the Captain's cane popped into his head. Captain Fearless—Chance Fortune. CF—CF. Had Captain Fearless known? It would've been just like the old rascal.

"Are you familiar with Captain Charles Fearless? Do you know his emblem?"

"My neural net contains access to every known superhero on file, beginning with Gilgamesh of the Assyrians—" MOTHER began.

"I'll take that as a yes," Chance said. "How about something like that, but small, here on the left side of my chest."

"Processing."

A modernized version of the Captain's trademark overlapping CF raised itself from Chance's suit in an emboss.

"Yeah—that's *just* right—*smooth*," Chance said, admiring both the emblem and his costume in its entirety.

"Now that your superhero identity is complete, I am equipping you with the final piece of your ensemble—the standard-issue Burlington communicator watch."

Chance looked on as a rather simple digital watch materialized around his gloved left wrist. He raised the watch to eye level. Holograms several times its size sprang from the watch face.

"As you may have guessed from its name," MOTHER said, "its primary function is as a communications device between yourself and all other Burlington associates. However, it is also uplinked to my neural net, granting you access to all the Academy's online resources."

"You've got to be kidding me," Chance said, watching as the holograms receded back into the watch. "What's next? Flight rings?"

"No," MOTHER said. "Flight rings are expensive, technologically advanced mechanisms, even by Burlington standards. They are only distributed to members of The Brotherhood of Heroes upon acceptance into that noblest of superhuman organizations. Few Academy graduates achieve the standards to be honored with membership or its gift."

Chance shook his head in disbelief. He was here. He was doing it. He was becoming an honest-to-goodness, living, breathing superhero. He couldn't wait to see what happened next!

7

Chance began to pace around the cubed room, performing various martial arts moves, testing his uniform's flexibility. "Fits like a dream, MOTHER. What do we do now?"

"In order to assess your skill level," MOTHER said, "we will now conduct an individual combat training session. Processing . . ."

Chance felt something slam into the back of his head. He fell facedown onto the floor. He looked up to see a silver boomerang circle through the air and disappear into one of the room's walls.

"Lesson one," MOTHER said. "Expect the unexpected."

"Now you tell me." Chance jumped to his feet as a large, sharp metal spike pierced the floor where his face had been only seconds earlier.

"Good," MOTHER said. "You learn quickly."

The grid lines around Chance shimmered. Suddenly, he

found himself standing in a dark New York alley at night. The walls around him were sprayed with graffiti. The concrete pavement beneath his feet was littered with trash soaking in rain puddles.

The floor beneath Chance expanded, the alley walls on either side rocketing apart, the distance between them now a city block. Then he rose into the air. Or rather, the ground beneath him did. The pavement shot upward, a gargantuan lift plank, carrying Chance to a height even with the surrounding skyscrapers. There it changed from ground to rooftop, taking on vents and air ducts and even a water tower, the terrain changing from concrete to tar, the alley floor now a building itself.

Something whizzed through the air at Chance's head. Acting on sheer instinct, he unsheathed one of the billy clubs holstered at his back, bringing it up before his face like a shield. The projectile lodged itself into the club's handle with a thunk.

Chance turned the club around to see a shiny throwing knife protruding from its end. He plucked it out, examined it, then looked up.

Ninjas dressed in black appeared all around Chance. They dropped from the water tower, flipped up out of air vents, and rolled out through the doorway leading up from the building. They wielded swords, knives, staffs, nunchakus, axes, spears, and clubs of every sort, and twirled them around their heads with grand mastery.

"Ninjas?" Chance asked, tossing the knife to the ground as

he reholstered his club. "You've got to be kidding me, right? I mean, this is right out of a bad 1980s action movie, MOTHER."

In response, the ninjas attacked from all sides, swords slashing, knives stabbing, nunchakus flailing. Chance flowed around them like water, bending under a spear point here, dodging under a sword swipe there. He was like an untouchable ghost in their midst.

"A swing and a miss," Chance said as a pair of nunchakus missed him and smacked another attacker on the head.

"Strike one." He rolled beneath a staff.

"Strike two." He slid between the spread legs of a sword-wielding ninja.

Chance somersaulted over three ninjas armed with knives. "Strike three!

"Three strikes," Chance said. "By my count, *you're all out!*"

With lightning speed, miniature silver Cs—personalized throwing projectiles, compliments of MOTHER—flew from Chance's fingers into his attackers. The tiny boomerangs knocked them unconscious.

He leapt atop their shoulders as they fell, pushing off with his feet to soar high into the air and then down into the crowd of their fellow shadow warriors.

When Chance landed, he held twin billy clubs. He used them to beat the ninjas, thumping skulls, necks, chests, and hands, disarming them and then taking them out altogether.

The remaining ninjas advanced. Chance attached the two billy clubs end-to-end. He pressed a button and the joined clubs extended to become a full-fledged bo staff. It whirred through the ninjas like a helicopter rotary blade, parrying swords, swiping legs, and again thumping skulls.

Chance detached the staff and reholstered its sections in one single smooth motion. There was one ninja left standing—Mr. Throwing Knife himself. Chance guessed this by the daggers lining the sash he wore across his torso.

He and Chance squared off like gunfighters in a spaghetti western. The knives came flying at Chance like horizontal rainfall. He backflipped the length of the roof, moving hands over feet, feet over hands until the barrage of daggers was depleted.

Chance came up at the roof's edge, unscathed, to see one last knife coming toward his face. He caught it by the blade and drew his arm back to throw it. Then, at the last moment, he hesitated. He flipped the knife in his hand so that he held its handle. Then he launched it. The dagger's blunt end struck its owner between his eyes. The ninja dropped to the ground, unconscious.

"You should have killed him," MOTHER said. "An opponent who lives is one who lives to fight another day."

"I will not kill simply because it's the convenient thing to do!" Chance said.

"You will not always have that luxury," MOTHER said.

"Perhaps."

Chance looked over the building's edge. The street was countless stories below.

"MOTHER," he said, "would you mind if I tried some swinging for a while? I haven't had a chance to test my grappling gun yet."

"That is acceptable," MOTHER said.

Before MOTHER could finish, Chance was over the edge, meteoring headfirst to the city street below, his arms and legs held tight at his sides.

Chance grinned as the ground rocketed up to meet him. *This is what it's all about,* he thought. *I'm going to love this life!*

He rolled in midair, unsheathed his grappling gun, and took aim at a gargoyle perched on the edge of a building. He fired.

Nothing happened.

Chance's eyes grew wide with terror. *What an idiot I am! I get to Burlington only to kill myself within my first hour here! I was a fool to think I could be a superhero!*

He was about to die and there was no avoiding it. He hit the ground and it gave beneath him, sinking down under his weight, sagging inward like a trampoline canvas.

"You have already forgotten your first lesson," MOTHER said. "Why were you certain your grappling gun would work? You had yet to test it."

"Point taken, MOTHER."

Chance sighed, got to his feet, and dusted himself off.

"Okay. Round two. Let's go!"

"Whoa, man! Cool threads!" Percy exclaimed as Chance stepped back outside the coliseum. "What do you think of mine?"

Percy looked like something out of a bad 1950s science fiction movie serial. He was clad in purple tights with white trim.

He wore a white plastic helmet and the image of a rocket surrounded by circling electrons sat on his chest. The costume stretched to impossible degrees over his roly-poly bulk.

Chance thought Percy's costume was quite funny, especially with the Coke-bottle glasses still riding his nose.

"Holy geez, pud! What are you supposed to be? Some kind of space cadet or something?" Shockley scoffed as he rejoined them.

"That's exactly right." Percy thrust out his chest and placed his hands on his hips. "I'm Space Cadet!"

"*Right,*" Shockley said. "Congratulations."

"Thanks!" Space Cadet said, beaming.

Chance looked at Shockley. Shockley was dressed the same as when he'd entered the coliseum.

"Couldn't find an outfit you liked, Shockley?" Chance asked.

"You can't improve upon perfection, boys," Shockley said. "By the way, it's Shocker now. Who's hungry?"

Chance's stomach grumbled at the mention of food. Breakfast seemed light-years past. "I'm starving. What about you, Per— Space Cadet?"

"I could eat a horse."

"I'd take that bet," Shocker said, grinning.

"Come on," Chance said, "I think McFarlane Cafeteria's back this way."

8

Chance, Shocker, and Space Cadet reached the McFarlane Cafeteria's rear entrance with a crowd of newly costumed freshmen. The cafeteria's door split in two and retracted within the walls to either side. Inside was an immense, octagonal stainless steel room. There were serving bars at each of the eight walls where droids took and dispensed food orders for the numerous students already gathered inside.

Chance recognized many of the faces from the courtyard. Like Space Cadet and himself—if not Shocker—they were now adorned in masks, capes, tights, and armor of every color of the rainbow.

Chance walked up to the bar with the shortest line. Shocker and Space Cadet went elsewhere to place their orders. When Chance's turn came, the portion of the bar before him retracted into the remaining surface to either side. A small tray popped up from the opening, and the bar pieces slid back into place beneath it.

"What may I serve you?" the servodroid behind the bar asked, his voice digitized and emotionless.

"What's on the menu?" Chance asked.

"Today's selection is Superaide with a choice of soylent yellow or soylent red," the servodroid said.

"That doesn't sound very appetizing. Do you have anything like soup? A sandwich maybe?"

"You may have either soylent yellow or soylent red. Both dishes are an artificially flavored, perfectly balanced nutritional supplement. Please place your order."

"Uh, soylent yellow, I guess," Chance said. The droid produced a small circular dish of white porcelain and placed a single yellow pellet on its surface. He set the plate and its cargo down on the tray and placed a cup of green liquid beside it.

"Thank you. Have a good day," the servodroid said.

Chance looked down at his lunch and then peered up at the robot in disbelief. "Are you kidding me?"

"Thank you. Have a good day," the servodroid repeated.

Chance walked away, sulking. *This certainly isn't Momma's home cooking.* He joined Shocker and Space Cadet at the serving room's exit and they walked into the cafeteria proper. McFarlane Cafeteria was a clear glass dome with beams of metal curving upward and joining at its apex. The Courtyard of Heroes was visible beyond the clear dome.

The cafeteria was already full of students sitting at the numerous rows of hoverchairs and hovertables. Above them, among the hoverlights, several large holograms broadcasted from hovering bulb projectors. They showcased superhumans in large-scale battles with one another, the spectacle far superior to any VR or holofilm special effects Chance had ever seen.

Chance felt someone shove by him and turned to see the Hawaiian-shirted boy striding past him, a winged superhuman following in his wake. *I see your manners haven't improved,* Chance thought. *Odd he's not outfitted yet. But then, neither is Shocker.*

"Where do you guys want to sit?" Space Cadet asked.

Chance looked down at Space Cadet's tray. Two cheeseburgers, an order of French fries, pizza, and cookies sat atop his plate in one gargantuan pile.

"How did you manage that, S.C.?" Chance asked, bewildered.

"S.C.," Space Cadet said. "I like that! But don't forget— I'm a technomancer. I just *told* the servodroids what I wanted and they gave it to me."

"Next time, pud, you do the ordering for all of us!" Shocker said. "As for the seating arrangements, I think I see some ladies who could use the company of three good-looking guys like us."

A few hovertables away, a striking redheaded girl with pale skin sat talking to an equally lovely six-armed East Indian girl.

"I-I-I-I'm not very g-g-g-good at talking to g-g-g-girls, Shocker," S.C. stuttered.

"Just be yourself." Shocker turned and looked down at Space Cadet. "Scratch that. Be anybody but you!" Then Shocker was off, walking toward his quarry's table. Chance shrugged and followed Shocker toward the girls' table. S.C. trailed after them hesitantly.

"Hello, ladies," Shocker said to the redhead and the Indian girl as he sat down across from them. "I'm Shocker." He extended his hand. "And you are?"

The redhead looked at Shocker's hand as though it were a snake. Then she looked up at his face, her jaw clenched, her eyes blue ice.

"Hi," Chance said to the pretty Indian girl. "I'm Chance. This is Space Cadet."

The girl folded all six of her arms and looked away, ignoring their presence. Chance shrugged at her dismissal, sat down, and ate his lunch in a single swallow.

"Are these mortals bothering you ladies?" a smug voice asked. "Say the word and I will kindly remind them to stay among their own kind."

Chance looked up to see a large boy towering over Shocker. He was dressed in a pair of sleeveless blue tights that revealed every ounce of his broad muscular physique. On his tan, knotted forearms, gauntlets of gold glistened above powerful clenched fists. A majestic cape of scarlet hung from his shoulders and a glittering sequined eagle sat upon his chest, its wings spread wide in perfect symmetry. He was square-jawed and blue-eyed. A single curled lock of blond hair drooped down from his overgelled hair to fall across his perfect, zitless forehead.

At the boy's left shoulder stood a tall, slender boy with spiked hair, sunglasses, and a full-length black trench coat. At his right shoulder stood another tall boy in a black devil suit with fiery red trim, cowl, and goggles. They both smiled hyena grins.

"Uh-oh," Space Cadet said.

"They were just leaving," the redhead said.

"Now wait a—!" Shocker said, rising to his feet.

"She's right," Chance said, grabbing Shocker by the arm, rising to stand beside him. "We were just leaving." He mumbled under his breath, "Come on, man, it's not worth it."

Shocker relaxed. He looked down at the redhead. "Don't worry, I'll call you," he said, smiling again.

Chance thought that whatever superpowers the redhead had, they must not have included laservision, for the look she gave Shocker would have sliced him in two otherwise.

Shocker stood and glared into the muscular boy's face, having to look upward to do so. Then he slid by, making sure to stare down both of the blond's cronies as he did so.

As Chance turned to grab his tray, he heard a loud crash behind him. He whirled around to see Space Cadet on his hands and knees tangled around the extended foot of the boy in the trench coat. The blond and his henchmen guffawed as they looked down at him.

Chance reacted. He pounced on Trench Coat, shoving him to the ground. Then he bent down to help Space Cadet to his feet.

"You okay, S.C.?" he said. But before S.C. could reply, Chance felt himself being hoisted into the air. He was spun around as though he weighed no more than a rag doll. Chance looked down to see the blond holding him by the throat.

The lights hovering above dimmed as though something was siphoning their power, then blue lightning jumped from Shocker's right hand toward the blond. Without taking his eyes off Chance, the blond raised his left hand, palm outward.

Shocker's discharge deflected harmlessly off it into the cafeteria's metal girders, where it dissipated.

"You," the blond boy said, his eyes turning red, "just made the worst mistake of your short, miserable life!" Chance gasped for air and pawed at the iron hand around his throat.

"Put him down, Superion," a deep, gravelly voice said.

"Says who?" the blond—Superion—asked without looking around.

"I do," the voice said, its tone now the rumble of an earthquake. The voice was attached to a huge, block-shaped thing. Its face sat in a rocky, square torso. Log-size arms sprouted from the torso where ears would be on a head. Its legs were short and jointless and made Chance think of petrified tree stumps.

"*Block*," Superion said. "I didn't see you there."

"Well, here I am!" Block said, his rocky brow making crunching noises as it furrowed. "Put him down. *Now.*"

"Sure," Superion said, setting Chance on his feet. "We were just having a little fun with the newbies. You know how it is." Chance collapsed to his knees, sucking sweet, pure oxygen into his lungs with large, hoarse gasps.

"Sure," Block said. "I know how it is."

"This isn't over, newbie!" Superion mumbled under his breath as he glowered down at Chance. "I won't have mortal trash strutting around all high and mighty! Not in my school!" Then he walked off, Trench Coat and Devil Suit in tow.

Shocker and Space Cadet stood staring at the human boulder before them.

"Why don't you see to your friend?" Block asked.

"Good idea!" Shocker said as he snapped out of his trance. He joined Space Cadet beside Chance. Chance was back on his feet, breathing easier.

"And here I thought I was going to be the brawler of the group!" Shocker punched Chance on his shoulder.

"Yeah, I really had him up against the ropes, didn't I?" Chance said, grinning back at him.

"You almost wore your butt for a hat!" Shocker said, laughing. "Thank goodness for the big guy here!"

"And speaking of," Chance said, as he, Shocker, and Space Cadet went over to the living mountain who'd saved him. "I owe you, man. Big time!"

"Don't mention it," Block said. "I saw them trip your friend. Superion and his team have won practically every battle they've fought here at Burlington, but he hasn't learned the first thing about what it means to be a hero." He extended one of his massive three-pronged clamps. "I'm Block, by the way."

"I'm Chance." Chance shook his hand. "This is Shocker and this is Space Cadet, S.C."

"Nice to meet you," Block said. "You guys want to sit over here with us?"

"Sure," Chance said.

They walked over to Block's table and squeezed in among five other students already sitting there.

"Guys," Block said, "this is Chance, Shocker, and Space Cadet."

"S.C.," Space Cadet corrected.

"This is Slug-Bug." Block gestured to a thin boy in blue-and-red short-sleeved tights.

Slug-Bug wore a mask that covered the upper portion of his face. Two large bulbs of plastic covered his eyes. Several smaller bulbs ran in twin lines up Slug-Bug's forehead until they terminated into two large sectioned antennae. These moved like actual living appendages. A red backpack and fingerless blue gloves completed his ensemble.

"Just your friendly neighborhood human-insect hybrid," Slug-Bug said, giving Chance and his friends a wave.

"We're Lost Boys," Block said.

"Excuse me?" Shocker asked.

"We're part of a battle team," Block said. "That's the biggest part of your education here at Burlington—learning to fight. Fight for yourself, fight with your team, fight against other teams. What do you think those holovids above you are?"

Chance, Shocker, and S.C. looked back up at the holograms playing throughout the cafeteria. As if on cue, a reel of Superion and his cronies sparring with a team of other super-humans began playing.

"Those are tapes from last year. We're sophomores, like your *friend,* Superion, and his boys, The Invincibles," Block said.

Chance didn't like the sound of that team name. He massaged his throat as he remembered the feeling of Superion's iron hand clamped around it. "Does every team fight every other team?" he asked.

"No," Slug-Bug said. "There's far too many. But there is a tournament at semester's end. The two teams with the best records go head-to-head and then the next two with the next-best records, and so on and so forth. The Invincibles made it to the finals our first semester—something unheard of for a freshman team—but were defeated by The Sensational Seven, a team of seniors."

"They had a perfect record the following semester," Block added.

"Without Superion, they'd be tough," Slug-Bug said. "With him, they're, well, invincible!" He frowned. "And they have a negator, too. With him around, your powers are null and void!"

"Now don't talk like that," Block scolded. "They haven't come up against The Lost Boys yet! And we've got something they don't have—teamwork. And that's worth all the Superions in the world!"

Massaging his throat, Chance hoped Block was right.

9

After lunch, they all exchanged good-byes as Chance, Shocker, and S.C. exited the cafeteria. They crossed the courtyard and headed toward the male dormitory section of campus. The dorms were identical needle towers that stood hundreds of stories above the ground. A windowed observation deck pinwheeled at the uppermost part of each tower.

"Which one are we again?" Shocker asked.

"Buscema," Chance answered. "It's two more down on the holomap."

They passed Silvestri and Swan and came to Buscema's outer door. A red square midway along the side of the door began to blink and MOTHER spoke.

"Please press your thumb here for access."

Chance did so and the door retracted up into the wall above it.

The tower's interior consisted of a circular tile floor, metal walls lined with chairs, and various holograms projecting down from the ceiling. Chance thought it looked like a waiting area, probably set up for visitors of Buscema's residents. Directly in the room's center, a clear lift tube ran up into the ceiling. The three boys walked over to the tube. An oval length of it slid open at their approach.

"Let's go upstairs and check out our rooms," Chance said.

They entered the tube and stood upon its circular lift plank. A hologram of buttons, one through three hundred in range, floated in the air at waist level. Chance checked the holomap and then keyed in their room numbers. The tube door slid back into place. The lift plank sprung to life, rocketing them upward. Chance felt gravity pulling at his face, turning his mouth into a frown as oval doors rushed past them like jumping film.

Their ride came to a jerking halt at Shocker's floor. A section of the tube folded over itself to form an opening. The opening was adjacent to a metal door with the number 98 stenciled upon it in gold. On the door a small square blinked with red light.

"Let's meet in the recreation deck, in, say, thirty minutes," Chance said. Shocker and S.C. nodded in agreement. Shocker pressed his thumb to the blinking red square and the oval door slid sideways into the adjoining wall. Shocker walked inside and the door to room 98 and the tube exit both slid back into place behind him.

The lift plank again jumped to life, bringing them to Chance's floor. Once again, there was an oval metal door, golden stencils, and a blinking red square. Chance pressed his thumb to the square, the door to his room, number 175, sliding open. He waved good-bye to Space Cadet, then walked inside his new living quarters.

The room was gleaming white, as if the floor, walls, and ceiling all exuded light. Chance threw his arm over his face to shield his eyes.

"Light output minimized twenty percent," MOTHER said.

Chance lowered his arm. The light was now a soft, yellowish off-white. "Thanks, MOTHER. You're in the dorm rooms, too?"

"You are welcome," MOTHER said. "And as I explained during your in-processing, my neural net consists of 563, 537, 676, 848, 478, 478 quantum bits spanning the known globe—"

"Okay, okay. Sorry I asked."

Chance looked about the room. It was a furnitureless semicircle. Two closet-size, rectangular blocks sprouted up from the floor back against the wall. Along one area, posters of rock 'n' roll bands and prominent superhumans hung like wallpaper. Apparently, Chance had a roommate who had already moved in.

"Would you like to sit down?" MOTHER asked as a portion of the wall slid open to produce a hoverchair. "Watch some holovision perhaps?" A hologram materialized in midair before the chair.

"Uh, no thanks," Chance said.

The wall opened once more. The chair retracted and the hologram terminated.

"It's been a long morning. Perhaps a bowel evacuation and a nap?" MOTHER asked as two more wall panels retracted. One produced a cryochamber standing on its end, the mattress visible through its clear glass housing. The other led to a small adjoining room. It housed what looked like a hi-tech torture device that used suction as its pain giver. Chance did need to urinate. Looking at the device, he decided he'd hold it for a while longer.

Twenty minutes later, Chance entered the recreation deck followed by Block. Around the deck, other boys boxed robotic opponents, shot zero-G billiards, checked and goaled at laser hockey, and played VR games of every possible description.

Chance saw Shocker had arrived ahead of them. "Hey, Shocker, guess who my roommate is."

"Heeeeeey," Shocker said, smiling as he slapped hands with Block. "Block! Good deal!"

"Guys! Guys!" Space Cadet exited the lift tube and came rushing over. "This is my roommate, Orson. He's a real live alien! Isn't that great?"

Accompanying S.C. was a tall, thin, green boy clad in a silver bodysuit. He glided, rather than walked, across the floor toward Chance and Shocker. Orson appeared as though he was from a planet in Xenoman's solar system. He was bald and had two tall, pointy antennae sprouting from his forehead. An occasional discharge of electric current snapped back and forth between them.

He slid up to Chance so they were separated only by mere inches and spoke. "Greetings I am Orson from the planet Shazzbot roommate of the humanoid called Space Cadet and second-year student here at Burlington Academy I look forward to social interaction with your person throughout the semester how are you called?"

"Uh, Chance." He took a step back only to have Orson once again close the distance between them. "Chance Fortune."

A jolt of electricity jumped between his antennae and Orson slid up into Shocker's face.

"Greetings I am Orson from the planet Shazzbot roommate of—"

"Whoa! Easy there, tiger!" Shocker said, pushing Orson back out of his face. "This is my space." He brought his arms together a foot and a half in front of his body. "You don't come within my space unless I ask you, and to be honest, you're not my type, follow me?"

The alien looked at Shocker, his head cocked to one side in confusion, electric current riding up his feelers.

Just then, a holographic image of Xenoman's head sprang out of each of their watches, his green cape collar an inverted cone around his bulbous purple head. "Greetings, freshman students," it said.

"Hey, look, Orson. Pa's calling," Shocker said, smirking.

"You're invited to the introductory gala beginning tonight at seven P.M. in McFarlane Cafeteria. Please come enjoy food, refreshments, and live entertainment while you meet and greet your professors, fellow classmen, and the Members of the Board."

The images vanished.

"Well," Chance said, "looks like we're going to a party, guys."

"Good thing, too," Shocker said. "I'm sure that redhead is dying to see me again!"

McFarlane Cafeteria had been opened up so that there was no barrier between it and the Courtyard of Heroes. Droves of students occupied both areas, sipping milky blue punch from Tupperware cups while they chatted and laughed and flirted.

Shocker ran to and fro on the lawn, pushing his way between bodies—scanning the courtyard for the icy redhead—while Chance, Space Cadet, and Orson followed him, chatting among themselves.

They made their way to the cafeteria, the music and lights coming from within intensifying as they advanced. Holograms of a rock band hovered in the air above their heads. Large masses of students gathered beneath these images, forming one many-headed, jumping, bouncing beast.

The hoverchairs and tables were gone. The rock band depicted in the courtyard's holograms floated on a saucer-shaped stage a few feet above the crowd. The cafeteria was a whirlwind of light, sound, and activity.

Chance stood watching, bobbing his head in time to the music. As he did so, a little green man, not two feet tall, dressed in a red leather jacket, criss-crossing spike-studded belts, and a single rhinestone glove moon-walked across the air in front of the band.

"If you want to stay," the little man said, "then you must play! I've got dancing feet, *so give me a beat!*"

The little green man snapped his fingers and the band played at faster and faster speeds. The little man spun like a top and reappeared dressed in baggy sequined balloon pants, jacket, and a pair of gaudy gold-rimmed sunglasses. Both the band's playing and his gyrating increased in ferocity until the music was gibberish and the little man a beating bee-wing blur.

The music crescendoed, then came to a screeching halt, huge pyrotechnics of smoke and flame exploding around the stage as the band members fell out from exhaustion. The little man stopped his dancing and rhymed to the crowd.

"Now that I've danced to a beat you can't touch—" He did another whirlwind spin to reappear in even larger gold-rimmed sunglasses, massive black sideburns, and a white sequined leisure suit complete with butterfly collar and minicape. "—I'll leave you by saying, 'Thank you, thank you, *ah thankyouverymuch!*'"

The little man hung his head, dropped to one knee, and held his arms and minicape out to his sides. All the lights within the cafeteria extinguished except for a spotlight shining down upon him. There was a high sucking sound, like an egg yolk passing through a straw, then the little green man disappeared with a loud pop.

"What—the hurl—was that?" Shocker asked.

"Oh, that's just Helix," a masked boy beside them answered. "He's an extradimensional."

"A what?" Chance asked.

"An *extradimensional*," the boy said. "You know, a sprite, a *djinn*—an imp from a supposedly higher dimensional plane.

He's kind of like the school's unofficial mascot. For the most part he's harmless. But pray he doesn't ever take a personal interest in you. Last year Professor Vanguard got fed up with Helix's antics and gave him a butt chewing. The professor spent the rest of the year teaching with a beach ball–size head."

Chance nodded in understanding and the masked boy turned his attention back to his own crowd.

"There she is," Shocker said, his face growing wide with a smile. The redhead from lunch stood several yards away flirting with a tall, handsome boy clad in a golden girdle and pharaoh headdress. She was now dressed in a black, armor-plated leotard, gauntlets, and boots of chrome metal. A silvery interlaced headband wove itself across her forehead, disappearing into her braided auburn mane.

"And some foreign Romeo is making his move!" Shocker said. "Flarn! Chicks are suckers for those types. You can't loan me some of that luck of yours, can you, Hicksville?"

"I'm afraid not," Chance said.

"Oh well, not like I need it anyway." Then Shocker was off to charm.

"Hey," Chance said, "isn't that Dr. Bryson over there?"

S.C. and Orson turned to look in the direction Chance had indicated. Dr. Adam Bryson stood a few yards away, signing autographs with a laser pen while he chatted with some of the students.

"Wow!" Space Cadet said. "Let's go talk to him!"

"You two go ahead, S.C.," Chance said. "I'm going to get some punch. I'll join you in a second." Space Cadet and his newfound alien sidekick were off without another word.

Chance made his way over to a nearby servodroid filling punch glasses. He took a cup and scanned the crowd.

He heard soft giggles behind him and turned to see a honey-skinned girl getting some punch with an insectoid girl. He did a double take.

The honey-skinned girl wore a costume of black leather much shinier than his own. Her emblem was a single glittering starburst at the center of her chest. She seemed to glow from within. Or that's how it seemed to Chance. He couldn't stop staring at her.

The insectoid girl was dressed in a costume of white. Her skin was newborn pink and her head was covered with short, stubbly silica rather than hair.

Chance cleared his throat and tried to speak. To his horror, he found all skills of language had left him. His throat closed up and refused to cooperate. He groped and struggled only to utter a few nonsensical syllables.

"I—uh—um—"

The insectoid girl grinned, the four pink nubby feelers of her mouth spreading wide beneath her large segmented blue eyes, and nudged her friend. The girl turned, finally taking notice of Chance. Her face was heart-stoppingly beautiful—huge dark eyes over a small delicate mouth and jaw.

"Yes?" she asked, her voice melodious, as she raised her eyebrows at Chance.

"I—ah—"

The girl cocked her head to one side and waited while Chance fumbled for words. Finally, she gave up waiting and shrugged, walking off with her girlfriend.

Chance was cursing himself when he felt someone grab him from behind. He was whirled around to find himself looking straight into the angry blue eyes of Superion.

"No rocky freak around to save you this time, newbie! Let's take a trip outside."

Superion turned and headed for the courtyard, dragging Chance behind him. The goggled boy in the black devil suit and the one in the trench coat walked in front of them, shoving bodies out of their way. They came to a little brown-headed boy in large spectacles who looked much too young to be attending the Academy and, out of sheer meanness, gave him an extra push for good measure.

The boy crumpled to the ground with a squeak, his Coke-bottle glasses falling off his face and shattering as they hit the cafeteria floor. Chance craned his head around as Superion dragged him toward the door. He saw the boy raise his head and glare at them with pupil-less, blood-red eyes.

"Why did you do that?" the boy asked.

Superion and the two other boys slowed, wheeling around to see who dared address them in such a fashion.

"Did you want to make me mad?" the boy asked. His voice had changed into a growl. When he spoke again it was an outright roar. *"YOU WON'T LIKE ME WHEN I'M MAD!"*

Chance, Superion, Devil Suit, and Trench Coat watched in horror as the little boy's face turned crimson. His head and jaw expanded, his skin bubbling and stretching. His arms and shoulders swelled into mountains beneath his crimson skin. The buttons popped from the boy's shirt as his increasing bulk ripped it to shreds.

In seconds, the boy had transformed into a twelve-foot-tall bull-roaring monstrosity. The other students screamed in terror as they trampled over one another in an attempt to flee the scene.

The thing moved with surprising speed, swatting Superion across the room as if he were a bug. Trench Coat and Devil Suit sprinted away. Chance rolled forward, just missing the impact of the thing's fist as it crashed through the floor where he'd been standing seconds before. The floor shook with the force of the blow. Chance was caught off balance and fell on his back.

The thing's apeish foot stomped across Chance's chest, knocking the wind from his lungs, pinning him to the floor. The thing raised one of its massive fists in the air and roared.

"Monstro, stop!"

It was the honey-skinned girl. She stood before the behemoth, her small delicate form a joke compared to its enormous and lethal bulk. Yet, the monster paused, his fist wavering uncertainly in the air above his head.

"Are you crazy?" Chance asked. "Get out of here!"

"NO!" the thing said to the girl. "STUPID BOYS PUSH MONSTRO! MONSTRO CRUSH! WHY THEY PUSH MONSTRO?"

The Board Members had now formed a circle around the scene. But they stopped and held their positions, watching this new development.

"I'm sure they're very sorry," the girl said. "Aren't you?" She looked down at Chance, her eyebrows raised high.

"But I didn't—" Chance said.

Justsayyou'resorry! she said in a desperate whisper. But her lips hadn't moved. Her voice had come from within Chance's own mind.

"Yeah," he said, nodding at Monstro. "I'm really, really, really sorry. It was an accident!"

"Ummmm," Monstro grunted, his face contorting as he mulled the apology over.

"See there, Monstro," the girl said. "He didn't mean it at all. You don't really want to crush anybody now, do you?"

"Monstro guess not," Monstro said, shrugging.

The girl went over to Monstro, taking his tree trunk–size arm with her own, stroking the monster's shoulder with her free hand.

"That's a good Monstro," she cooed. Monstro grinned, a guttural purr in his throat. He began to shrink. His skin lightened from red to shades of pink and then peach. At last, it was the little brown-haired boy who stood before the girl, his pants ragged tatters about his waist.

Alpha-Man walked up to them.

"Miss," Alpha-Man said, "would you mind coming with me to walk Simon back to his room? I think he's had enough excitement for the night."

"Not at all," she said, her arm around the boy's shoulders. "Would you like to go back to your room, Simon?" He nodded approval and then the three of them walked out toward the courtyard.

"Are you all right, young man?" Dr. Bryson asked as he helped Chance to his feet. S.C. and Orson stood behind him.

"Uh, yeah," Chance said. "I'm fine."

Shocker joined them.

"Flarn, man!" Shocker said. "For someone who has good luck as a power, you seem to attract a lot of trouble!"

Xenoman turned and addressed the students, who were now creeping back inside. "Everything is all right now, students," he said. "We'll have some music on for you in a moment. Please, everyone continue enjoying yourselves. Everything's fine. No need to worry."

Minutes later, the party was back in full swing. Xenoman made his way through the crowd, occasionally stopping to sign autographs. For the most part, he just walked and watched, making sure everything was running smoothly.

Then a small blond boy in a Hawaiian shirt caught his eye. The boy was standing just outside the walkway between McFarlane Cafeteria and Grant VR Library. He made eye contact with Xenoman and grinned slyly. The boy beckoned for the dean of students to follow him. Then he turned and ran down the walkway.

Curious, Xenoman followed. He reached out for the boy's thoughts with his mind, but nothing was there. Well, something was there. Memories of the boy's childhood, his family, his home. But they were playing repeatedly, like a skipping record. It was extremely odd.

Xenoman found the boy midway down the path. He closed the distance between them so they only stood a few feet apart. The boy stood immobile, surrounded by several other students, all of them stock-still and wearing the same sly grin as the boy. Xenoman surveyed their minds. More skipping records.

Their thoughts made Xenoman think of the old Earth movie thrillers he loved so much. The ones where cat burglars snuck looping videotapes into monitor rooms so they could go about their business unnoticed by security. Xenoman considered trying to push through this thought barrier, but the dean truly loathed such invasions of others' privacy, especially where his students where concerned. He decided upon a more direct approach.

"What's going on here?" Xenoman asked.

The blond boy opened his Hawaiian shirt in response and darkness enveloped the alien dean.

10

"Your individual combat training is concluded for the day," MOTHER said. "It is now time for you to report to your team combat training session."

After the hectic events of the previous night, Chance had been pleased to have a rather uneventful first morning of classes. The six o'clock calisthenics with the half-man, half-tiger Professor Claw had cleared his head so he was ready to learn in his eight o'clock class, Superhuman Diplomacy, with the empathic Professor Goodvibe. The dean of students, Professor Xenoman, had lectured on the Amazonian scrolls regarding the psychology of warfare in Chance's nine o'clock class, Theory of Superhuman Battle Tactics. Next had been Chance's favorite class, Superhuman History 101 with the talking, genius gorilla Professor Claremont. Now, after a break for lunch and his ICT, or individual combat training, Chance was looking forward to finding out who his battle teammates would be in his last class of the day, Team Combat Training.

Chance stood there a moment, panting and exhausted from his two-hour workout. To his right, the wall opened to reveal a long hallway leading into the depths of Kirby Coliseum.

"Please exit through the space provided," MOTHER said.

He followed MOTHER's directions until he came to an area that defied description. Chance had entered an infinity of phosphorous mist. It was like standing in an ocean of thunderheads.

A series of platform rings laid out like a horizontal dartboard hovered motionless in the mist before Chance. The rings were intersected by criss-crossing walkways. A large circular platform sat at the center of the rings. Atop it were twin monoliths. Chance watched as strobes of purple energy climbed the monoliths to discharge at their apexes. *Those look like Tesla coils on steroids!*

Chance looked skyward and noticed the humongous, weaving metal rings that circled the entire structure like an enormous gyroscope.

What is this place? Could it be a VR simulation? Chance didn't think so. How could it exist even in that form when by doing so it violated every natural law? It was beyond all logic and reason.

He gasped as Steel Valkyrie appeared in all her Viking glory on the central platform, teleporting in with a blaze of light. "Greetings, Chance Fortune," she said. "You are the first of your team to arrive for team combat training. Please come join me on the center platform."

Chance looked down and saw a lightning bolt flash inside the bottomless mist. *Couldn't there at least be handrails?* he thought.

"No need to be frightened," Steel Valkyrie said. "Just keep on the straight path and you will be fine."

Despite his expert coordination and Steel Valkyrie's reassurance, Chance took one timid step forward and hesitated. Leaping from tall buildings and beating down ninja armies he could handle, but the unknown filled him with fear.

"*Mach schnell!*" Steel Valkyrie snapped. "Hurry up!"

Chance gulped and inched along the walk, not daring to look up or down or to his sides, keeping his gaze focused on Steel Valkyrie. Halfway there, he thought about the swirling depths below, and how if he were to go over the side he'd fall and fall and fall for eternity. He wavered, teetering on the abyss's edge, the world pinwheeling around him.

"*Guten Tag,*" Steel Valkyrie said. "You must be Psy-chick."

Chance steadied himself enough to look up and see the honey-skinned girl from the party standing on the outermost platform. The girl—Psy-chick—looked at him from the entry-way and smiled. She was clad in her black, snug-fitting costume with the white starburst emblem. She crossed the walkway and stood on the center platform.

Not wanting to look like a coward in front of Psy-chick, Chance made it the rest of the way down the walkway with limited difficulty.

"Glad you could join us," Steel Valkyrie said, frowning.

"Simon—" Psy-chick smiled at Chance. "I mean *Monstro*— wanted you to know he's sorry."

"Uh, yeah, uh . . ." Chance said, blushing. "I never got to thank you last night. For saving me, I mean. You were incredible! I'm—"

"Chance Fortune," Psy-chick said. "I know. I'm a *psionic*."

"What's a psi-onic?" Chance asked, hoping his face didn't give away the apprehension he was feeling. If it meant what he thought it did, the secret of his true identity was in peril!

Steel Valkyrie looked at her communicator watch and shook her head. "Where could your teammates be? I abhor tardiness!"

Psy-chick waited several seconds to see if Steel Valkyrie had anything further to say. Satisfied the professor was finished, Psy-chick continued her conversation with Chance. "I'm a telepath. And an empath, both receptive and projective. A low-level telekinetic, too. I've tried pyrokinesis but haven't had much luck."

"You can invade minds?" Chance asked, his fears all but confirmed.

"Invade?" she asked. "The problem is keeping other people's thoughts out!"

Psy-chick gave Chance a suspicious look, her large, lovely brown eyes gazing intently into his. "Everyone's but yours, that is. I can tell you're tense right now, but all I get from you on the thought level is the occasional name or word."

Chance breathed a sigh of relief. The secret of his normalcy was safe—for the present. Then there was a slight tingle at the base of his skull, a flittering, no more than the gentle brush of a dove's wing.

"When I reach out to you—I hit—well, a brick wall. How do you do that?"

"Stop it!" Chance said. "Get out of my head!"

Psy-chick jumped and took a step back. A pink blush spread across her cheeks.

"I'm so sorry," she said, staring down at the platform. "I didn't mean any harm. It's just I've never met anyone who didn't broadcast before."

Chance put his hand to her shoulder. It was soft and warm. He wanted to leave his hand there forever. Psy-chick looked down at Chance's hand in surprise, but did not draw away.

"It's okay," he said and then, using every ounce of willpower at his disposal, removed his hand. "It was really—kind of nice."

"Finally!" Steel Valkyrie interrupted. "Another arrival! Greetings, Mr. Shocker."

Chance looked over his shoulder to see Shocker joining them on the platform.

Ignoring Chance, Shocker gave Psy-chick a mischievous smile, lowered his sunglasses, and winked at her with one electrical eye. "I'm Shocker," he said. "And I'm *very* pleased to make your acquaint—!" Suddenly, Shocker tripped over his own feet and fell into Chance. Chance caught his friend and righted him.

"Very smooth!" Psy-chick laughed.

"Hello there," Steel Valkyrie said. "And you, of course, must be Gothika. Come join your teammates on the platform."

Gothika was a girl dressed entirely in black. Various silver rings rode atop her tattooed fingers and pierced her ears, navel, eyebrows, and nose. A silver Egyptian ankh hung down across her chest, suspended on a silver circular band. Her ankh began to glow silvery white. Then she glided across the walkway onto the platform on the tips of her toes.

No doubt about her powers, Chance thought. *Gothika's a witch!*

"Hey, guys!"

It was Space Cadet. He came running down the platform waving with glee, a purple-and-white butterball. He stopped halfway and put his hands on his knees, catching his breath.

"Hello, Space Cadet," Steel Valkyrie said. "Please hurry and join us on the platform."

"Hey, guys—" S.C. said, panting as he reached the others. "We're—all—on the same—team—cool!"

"Ah, here we are," Steel Valkyrie said. "Greetings, Private Justice."

"Ma'am! Private Justice reporting for TCT, ma'am!"

Private Justice wore a bright red and blue costume. An image of balanced scales was sewn across his chest. Chance thought if America's Uncle Sam had a real nephew, Private Justice would be it.

"Oh no," Shocker said.

"What?" Chance asked.

"That tightwad is my roommate! He's been spouting rules and regulations at me since last night! I can't take this, Hicksville!"

Private Justice came to a halt before Steel Valkyrie. He raised his arm and it wound around his body several times before reaching his brow to snap off a salute.

Wow! Chance thought. *He has the power of elasticity!*

"Oh, you gotta be kidding me!" Shocker said. He turned to Steel Valkyrie. "Ma'am, there's got to be some mistake. There's no way Dudley Do-Right here could be on our team. I mean, it just isn't possible! Either he goes or I go!"

"There must be some mistake!" a flinty voice exclaimed.

It was the redheaded girl from the party. She stormed down the walkway, her cheeks as crimson as her hair, her armor-plated leotard clanking with her every step.

"I shouldn't be with these—*mortals*! Especially not this one!" She looked in Shocker's direction, grimacing with disgust.

"I take back everything I said," Shocker said, his face full of glee. "Serving on this team will be both an honor and a privilege!"

"You can't expect me to deal with their kind!" The redhead stomped her booted foot down on the platform. It shook from the force of impact, rocking Chance and the others on their feet.

"Wow!" S.C whispered to Chance. "She's got superstrength!"

"How am I—?" the redhead started to say.

"*Silence!*" Steel Valkyrie shouted, the sound of distant thunder mingling with the echo of her voice. "All of you!" Everyone snapped to attention. Steel Valkyrie let them all feel the full weight of her gaze before letting it come to rest on the redhead.

"MOTHER compiles the battle teams using an algorithm composed by Dr. Bryson himself," Steel Valkyrie said. "It takes into account the various personalities, experiences, and abilities of all the Burlington students and then organizes them into compatible groups of seven. There has been *no* mistake. The system is flawless. Is that clear?"

Hmmm, Chance thought. *We've got magic with Gothika, electricity with Shocker, technomancy with S.C., elasticity with Private Justice, physical strength with the redhead, and mind power with Psychick. Steel Valkyrie's right. Sounds like a well-balanced team. Expect for me, that is, of course. I don't have any powers at all.*

Steel Valkyrie once again looked at each of them in turn, making sure all doubts about their team placement and her authority were quelled. "Good. As you all know, I am Steel Valkyrie of The Brotherhood of Heroes, head shield maiden of the Asgardian Realm. I will be serving as your TCTI, or team combat training instructor, this semester."

From the corner of his eye, Chance saw the redhead roll her eyes at Steel Valkyrie's last sentence.

"You will meet here within Kirby Coliseum's Infinity Chamber every afternoon for transport to our training locale for the day."

"You mean this is another teleportation chamber?" Space Cadet asked.

"Not quite," Steel Valkyrie said. "The Infinity Chamber folds space and time around its occupants. It creates a doorway between dimensions. This allows us to move to anywhere within the *multiverse.*"

"Multiverse?" Chance asked.

"The multiverse encompasses all known universes," Steel Valkyrie said, "both those parallel to our own and those . . . *not so parallel.*

"Moving to other realities for TCT helps cut down on the wear and tear we superhumans inflict upon the coliseum during ICT."

Steel Valkyrie made a sweeping gesture with her arms at the phosphorous mist swirling about them. "What you see around you is the nexus between universes—or dimensions, if you prefer. Like much of the nexus, this area has Earth-type gravity and atmosphere.

"The navigational aspect of the Infinity Chamber is controlled by MOTHER. She draws upon coordinates and data gathered from hundreds of thousands of previous expeditions. The warping of space and time itself is accomplished by the Infinity Posts you see here before you." Steel Valkyrie motioned to the twin monoliths pulsating with purple energy, then continued her speech.

"I cannot stress it upon you enough to keep clear of them when activated. For someone like Freyja—I mean, Iron Maiden," Steel Valkyrie said, gesturing at the redhead, "—or myself, being caught between the posts during the warping process would be quite devastating. For mortals like the rest of you, it would be terminal."

Chance heard S.C. gulp.

"All TCT consists of three main scenarios," Steel Valkyrie continued. "Last Team Standing, Snatch and Grab, and Random.

"Last Team Standing is the most commonly used scenario, and typically the most difficult, as it reflects the real-world situation superheroes usually find themselves in—combat with supervillains.

"During Snatch and Grab sessions, you will be provided with an objective, typically some item you must procure from your opponent team's base, and then successfully smuggle it to your own while defending against the opposing team from accomplishing the same goal."

"Like capture the flag," Private Justice said.

"More or less," Steel Valkyrie said. "The third and final scenario is Random, and it is exactly that. It can be a combination of the other two scenarios, or something else entirely. All scenarios will increase in difficulty throughout the course of the semester. For example, a simple Last Team Standing bout might be complicated by the injection of other outside factors."

"Like what?" Shocker asked.

"Well," Steel Valkyrie said, "that, as you mortals say, is for me to know and for you to find out.

"Before we begin, a team captain must be assigned. It should be someone capable of giving orders and coordinating team maneuvers, both offensive and defensive. Would anyone like to volunteer?"

Private Justice jumped up and down, waving his arms in the air. "Oh, I do, ma'am. I do! Pick me! Pick me!" Everyone else simply stood in silence.

"Iron Maiden, then," Steel Valkyrie said, a hint of reproach in her voice. "She is the daughter of *two* great warriors, after all. And certainly the most powerful among you. Her being leader is the natural course of things."

Private Justice kicked at the platform and shook his fists. "Not fair! Not fair!"

"Aw," Shocker whispered as he mimed wiping tears from his eyes, "poor little teacher's pet!"

"Fine!" Iron Maiden said, haughtiness radiating from her.

"I'll be team captain. I would never accept orders from a mortal anyway!"

"Excellent," Steel Valkyrie said. "Before team competition begins next week you must all decide upon a team name. So be thinking about it throughout the course of the week. "Now, if everyone would step back from the posts, I shall warp us to our training locale for the day."

Steel Valkyrie waited until everyone had made their way out from between the Infinity Posts to the platform's edge. "Somewhere in the Vegan system should do nicely, I think." She reached toward the control panel located at shoulder level on the side of the right post. She punched a series of keys— coordinates, Chance thought—and pressed a green, diamond- shaped button larger than the rest at the control panel's bottom.

Torrents of purple energy leapt between the Infinity Posts. There was a blinding purple-white flash and then they were no longer within the Infinity Chamber. Only the two Infinity Posts remained as proof they'd ever been there. But now, the twin monoliths rose from a barren brown landscape. It was a flat plane that stretched off into the distance beneath a green sky as far as the eye could see. As far as Chance's human eyes could see anyway.

The Infinity Posts opened and several small cameras floated into the sky to cover their battle.

"So begins your first TCT," Steel Valkyrie said. "I shall simply observe from afar. Good luck to you all." She strode to the Infinity Posts, pressed a button on her communicator watch, and disappeared in a flash of light.

"So what now?" Shocker asked. "This ain't so—"

At that moment, a circle of dust exploded from the ground around them. When the dust cleared, several dozen shiny, thin robots marched forward, closing in around Chance and his teammates.

11

"ATTACK!" Iron Maiden roared as she leapt at the droids closest to her. She plowed through them like a hurricane, shattering the robots to pieces.

Shocker didn't need anyone to tell him twice. He removed his black sunglasses. The electrical fire burning within him shot out of his eye sockets and leapt across the bridge of his nose. "Let's light it up!" he said. Bolts of blue lightning jumped from his hands and eyes to short-circuit several advancing robots.

"*Morf tsud uoy emac dna ot tsud uoy llahs nruter,*" Gothika chanted. The three robots closing in on her paused and then crumbled into large piles of dust.

"Prepare to receive Justice!" Private Justice bellowed as he waved his finger in the air. From the way he said it, Chance thought he'd probably been practicing it in the mirror for weeks.

Private Justice elongated his torso, snaking it around several of the robots. Then he squeezed the robots into a single mass like a python squashing its prey. There was a sizzle of sparks and the robots' eye lights expired.

Chance turned to see Space Cadet kneeling on the ground. S.C.'s back was to him, but Chance saw his little roly-poly friend reach out every so often and grab a random robot part from the pile of debris left in Iron Maiden's wake.

When S.C. got up, Chance saw that his teammate had constructed some type of vehicle from the robot parts. It looked like an oversize pogo stick. Space Cadet grabbed the robot forearms serving as handlebars and stepped on the robot feet that served as its base. S.C. pushed a button on the vehicle's control panel and both he and the contraption rose high into the air. A red laser beam fired out the vehicle's makeshift mast and zapped several of the remaining robots. Chance saw a grin of delight across S.C.'s face.

"Look out, Chance!" Psy-chick yelled.

Chance ducked as a free-floating robot arm whizzed through the air above his head to pelt a robot that had been sneaking up behind him. Psy-chick held out her hand and concentrated, battering the robot with her telekinetically controlled bludgeon until its eyes went dark and it crumpled to the ground.

"That's two I owe you!" Chance said.

Psy-chick grinned and winked in response.

Another robot made for Chance, its arms outstretched. He ducked beneath them and punched the robot's metal chest cavity. The impact produced a loud thunking sound. Chance retreated, shaking his hand, his face a grimace of pain. *Well, that didn't work out so well,* he thought. The robot continued to advance. Chance leapt into the air and landed a roundhouse kick to its head, setting it spinning like a top. The robot reached up and took hold of its chrome dome to stop the rotation.

As it did so, Chance noticed two openings under its arms. Chance reached inside an opening and yanked out a fistful of wires. The robot fell lifeless.

Now that's more like it!

Chance dispatched the last few functioning robots, kicking them in the head, setting them spinning. They'd reach for their rotating heads only to have Chance rip out a handful of their innards, putting them out of commission. Minutes later, the barren terrain was once again free of operating droids.

"Well," Shocker said, "that wasn't so tou—"

Before he could finish, another batch of droids exploded up from the ground. Then another, and another.

"Would you keep your mouth shut?" Gothika yelled to Shocker.

Here we go again, Chance thought as he spin-kicked a robot head.

On it went, batch after batch of robots sprouted, more and more of them appearing until Chance and his teammates were surrounded by a sea of robots intent on pounding them into oblivion.

They'd been battling for over an hour. Chance looked to his teammates. Shocker's blasts now issued with less and less potency. Psy-chick was grimacing with effort, her flying robot-arm club now sluggish and weak. Gothika was reduced to defensive measures. She sat within the safety of a perpetual ring of flame, her efforts to down droids long ceased.

Private Justice had inflated himself into the protective shape of a round balloon. Robots bounced off him, gripping for handholds but finding none. But no robots fell by his hand. Even Iron Maiden now attacked with less ferocity. Chance thought he even saw a trickle of sweat running down the back of her neck.

Other than Chance, only Space Cadet lacked any signs of fatigue. He still flew around the battlefield blasting robots with his makeshift hovercraft. But it was obvious from the indifferent expression on S.C.'s face that he'd descended into boredom.

This is getting us nowhere, Chance thought as he maneuvered through the inanimate drones piled at his feet. *And it's only a matter of time before we all give out and these robots overrun us.*

"S.C.," Chance said. The smart chips in his communicator watch beeped as they recognized his intent to speak with Space Cadet and opened a channel between the two students.

"This is S.C. What's up, Chance?"

Chance roundhoused a robot's head.

"These robots don't seem to be much more than automatons. Do you think there's a chance they might be operating on a central intelligence?"

Space Cadet puttered about in the air, picking off robots with his laser beam.

"That's a correct assumption, Chance. They're operating on a single signal, probably broadcasting from beneath the ground since that's where they're coming from. I'm not sure. I couldn't get a fix. But I'm sure about the signal. They all have receiver chips in their heads. At least the ones Iron Maiden crashed through, anyway."

Chance yanked a fistful of wires from a robot's chest cavity.

"Can you construct something to block it? Jam the signal?"

"I think so. I never thought to do it. It was just so much fun blasting them at first. But Iron Maiden told us to attack, and I certainly don't want to disobey her. She might decide to crush me instead of the robots!"

Chance ducked under the grasping arms of a robot.

"I'll think she'll concede on this one, S.C. And if something goes wrong, don't worry. I'll take full responsibility. Get down here, man. I'll protect you while you put something together. Chance out."

"Shocker," Chance said, his communicator watch once again beeping to life.

"Yo! I'm a little busy here!"

Chance put another robot out of its misery.

"Get your electric butt over here. S.C.'s gonna cook something up to get us out of this mess. He needs our cover."

"On my way."

Moments later, they both reached Chance. Space Cadet landed and set to work, Chance and Shocker shielding him from the attacking droids.

The robots closed in around them. Across the horde of droids, Chance saw Private Justice being twisted into knots by the robots. Both Gothika and Psy-chick were being carried in the air by robotic arms, their defenses overcome. Chance caught a glimpse of red hair among a moving heap of robots and thought Iron Maiden must be somewhere inside, still punching and kicking, but to no avail.

The robots now covered Chance and his friends. Chance and Shocker dispatched droids with frantic desperation.

"Pud," Shocker called as he deflected grasping robot arms, "whatever you're going to do, you better do it now!"

Robots clawed at Chance's face. He felt arms of cold steel hoist him into the air. His grappling gun was ripped from its holster. One of the drones wadded it into a ball of scrap metal. Chance looked over and saw Shocker also being hoisted into the air.

"S.C.!" Chance cried.

"Just a few more seconds!" S.C. yelled.

"Pud," Shocker yelled, "in a few more seconds, we're going to be human pretzels!"

"*Mmmm,*" S.C. said as he rubbed his ample belly. "Pretzels."

"PERCY!" Chance cried.

The robots froze. Their eye lights blinked out. All of them. Then they tipped over, falling on themselves like huge metal dominoes.

Chance and Shocker dropped, Chance landing on his feet, Shocker on his butt.

"What happened?" Psy-chick asked, stumbling over fallen droids as she came toward them, Gothika not far behind her.

A heap of robots exploded in a shower of silver arms and legs to reveal Iron Maiden. She leapt the length of a football field, coming to land near the rest of the group.

"*Was ist das?*" she asked, peering behind Chance and

Shocker to where Space Cadet stood, a smile beaming from his pudgy face, a metal contraption made from droid parts at his feet. It made bleeping noises as waves of energy exuded from it to jam the robots' control signal.

"You did it, Pud!" Shocker said. "I don't believe it, but you actually did it!"

Psy-chick made her way between Chance and Shocker to give Space Cadet a big hug. "Way to go, S.C."

"It was Cha—" S.C. started to say. Chance gestured for him to keep quiet. He pointed at S.C. and gave him a thumbs-up.

Space Cadet grinned back at him. What Psy-chick did not catch of this from the corner of her eye, she read in Space Cadet's mind. She looked at Chance, an admiring smile across her face.

12

"It's about time!" Iron Maiden snapped.

"Sorry," Chance said as he joined the rest of his teammates in one of Grant VR Library's study rooms. It was the day after their first practice battle. He sat down at the circular hovertable. A large hologram rotated in the air above the table. It read:

THE INVINCIBLES vs. tHe LoSt BoYs
Match, Last Team Standing

The Invincibles's moniker was displayed in broad block letters that shot out at the reader and glistened as if they were gold bathed in light. The Lost Boys's moniker alternated between lower- and upper-case letters and was scripted in a neogothic style.

"Now, why are we watching this?" Gothika asked as she

removed her leather jacket and hung it on the back of her hoverchair.

"To learn." Iron Maiden tossed her long auburn hair. "Mortals like you need to study your opponents in order to be successful!"

Gothika stood and pointed a rune tattoo–covered finger at Iron Maiden. "The rest of us may just be mutants, magicians, and lab accidents, but you can't talk to us like that!"

"I think what Iron Maiden was trying to say is—" Psy-chick began.

"Oh, I know exactly what she was trying to say!" Gothika said as she and Iron Maiden glared at each other.

"Going to be a good one." Shocker fastened his bandanna about his head. He spared a quick glance at Chance and then returned his attention to the hologram. "Blockhead and 'Bug will give 'em what for!"

"I doubt it," Private Justice said, his brow furrowing beneath his blue mask. "I've never seen a more undisciplined character than Slug-Bug. Well, except for you, that is!"

"Watch yourself, beanpole!" Shocker said.

"Cool it, guys," Chance said. "It's starting."

Before them, the hologram scattered into a thousand tiny dots of light and then re-formed to display both The Lost Boys and The Invincibles squaring off in an ancient Roman arena. In addition to the two opposing teams, numerous robot gladiators and fierce alien predators scampered about the arena, hacking and slashing, biting and clawing at any Burlington student unlucky enough to cross their path.

Block made his way through the arena's obstacles toward Superion.

"Smart move," Psy-chick said.

"I wouldn't go after Superion!" Space Cadet said. "He's the toughest one out there!"

"Ha," Chance said. "Not against Block. His achillesheelenite skin is toxic to Superion."

"Achilleswhatchamahuh?" Shocker asked.

"Ah-kill-eez-heel-en-nite," Chance said, sounding out the word. "Block told me all about it. Because his skin is made of it, Superion gets sick if he comes within ten feet of him!"

"Quite the tactical advantage, then!" Iron Maiden said.

"Come on, Block," Chance said as he watched the hologram from the edge of his seat. "Get him!"

But Chance's wish was thwarted as a massive elephantlike creature plowed into Block from behind. The creature then proceeded to stomp Block senseless into the arena floor.

"Oh no!" Space Cadet exclaimed.

"Block may be down," Chance said, "but he's not out!"

As if he'd heard Chance's words, Block sprang up from the ground and grabbed the six-legged, three-trunked mastodon and threw it across the arena. Then he charged Superion once more. Just as Block was about to reach him, the Invincible known as Raz, a negator who looked like a vampire, and Speed Demon, the devil-suited speedster, tackled him to the ground. Chance winced as he watched the two Invincibles beat at The Lost Boys captain. Block struggled against them, but his superstrength had been negated, thanks to Raz's presence.

"Hey, no fair!" Private Justice jumped to his feet, his fists clenched.

"Those guys think everything's fair, P.J.," Psy-chick said. "Even when they cheat!"

Chance and his teammates watched glumly as the remaining Invincibles continued to stay one step ahead of The Lost Boys. Chance recognized the Invincible known as Mindbender, a telekinetic, from their confrontation in the cafeteria. His teammate, the wererat Ratticus, was every bit as filthy and sniveling as his name implied. But Warlock was the strangest of them all. His body was literally the void of space in human form. Tiny comets streaked across the wizard adept's chest and pint-size galaxies swirled in his arms and legs.

Across the arena from Block, the Lost Boy and plant creature known as Creeper sat at the feet of the whip-wielding Invincible known as Delilah. Despite her beauty, Chance thought Delilah looked quite menacing in her outfit of form-fitting black leather—especially in comparison to Creeper's small, vegetation-composed body. Delilah's whip was wound around Creeper's green neck as though it were a leash.

"Why doesn't Creeper do something?" Gothika asked.

"It's Delilah's whip," Psy-chick said. "If she wraps it around you, she can control your mind. And if that's not bad enough, she's a shape-shifter, too."

On the hologram, Superion flew across the arena to join Delilah. He gave Delilah a malicious smile and then turned his attention to Creeper.

"Well, well," Superion said. "What do we have here? An annoying little weed?"

"Answer him!" Delilah snarled.

"Yes," Creeper said, unable to help himself, "I'm a no-good weed."

"Weeds pollute the flowerbed," Superion said. "They must be pulled out—eradicated."

"Yes," Creeper agreed, a single tear rolling down his mossy face, "I must be eradicated."

At that moment, Block kicked and punched Speed Demon and Raz off him and went after Superion.

"I'm glad you agree," Superion said. "You see, I can't allow the fight to continue. As much as I hate to admit it, with Block and his achillesheelenite hide around, you might actually win. Anyway, this is going to be much harder on me than it is you." He paused and then laughed. "Well, not really."

Creeper screamed in agony as Superion activated his laser vision and blasted him. His body burst into flames.

Chance and his teammates gasped in disbelief, watching wide-eyed and open-mouthed at the horror being played out before them.

"NO!" Block shouted. He brought his hands together in a thunderous clap. The resulting shockwave knocked Superion, Delilah, and Creeper off their feet. The action also snuffed out the flames crawling across his teammate's body, leaving Creeper a crumpled, charred mass against the arena wall.

Block rushed to Creeper's side. "MOTHER! End the fight! End the fight now!"

"The TCT battle cannot be terminated until a victor is declared or its time limit expired."

"We yield!" Block pleaded. "The Lost Boys yield! End it! We have to get Creeper home! Now!"

The hologram disintegrated into thousands of tiny dots of light and then re-formed itself into the words

WINNER,
THE INVINCIBLES

Chance and his teammates stared at one another. For once, even Shocker was speechless.

The next day, Chance stood with Block at Creeper's bedside in the campus clinic.

"Hey, man," Block said. He extended a ham-size fist to Creeper. In the clinic's sterile metal room, a hologram of Creeper's X-ray floated above them, showcasing the nanite machines working tirelessly to repair the Lost Boy's wounds. Thanks to both the Burlington clinical staff and his own powers of self-regeneration, Creeper's burns were well on their way to healing completely.

Creeper's yellow eyes fluttered half-open and the vines composing his arms wrapped themselves around Block's hand.

The door slid open and a masked female nurse poked her head inside.

"Time's up, boys," the supernurse said. "Let's let Creeper rest a while."

They said their good-byes and then the boys made their way outside.

"Creeper's lying in there like *that* and Superion only got a week's detention!" Chance said. "That's not even a slap on the wrist!"

"I'll bet it's because of his father," Block said, staring off at the horizon, anger in his voice. "Supremeus is a large financial contributor to the school. Their family has been coming here for ages. Superion's a legacy and then some. Not a flarn thing's going to happen to him." He walked off to class.

Chance stared at the ground. He thought about his first meeting with Superion, Superion's grip around his throat, how he'd massaged his throat in fear—fear of Superion—and was ashamed. And now Creeper lay only half-alive in his clinic bed. Chance gritted his teeth.

Well, I'm not going to be ashamed anymore. No. From now on, I'm going to be angry!

Chance clenched his first and spoke out loud. "I promise, no, I swear—I swear with everything that I am, within the reach of my arm, the world will not be that way! Within the reach of my arm, the Superions of the world will not prosper!"

Moments later, Chance was roaming the hallways of Lee Old Main trying to find his next class.

"I was just in Professor Claremont's class yesterday!" Chance muttered to himself. "How could I have gotten so lost? Maybe it's downstairs?" He came to a lift plank and groaned when he saw it was out of order. But there was a staircase at the end of the corridor. "Guess it's the old-fashioned way, today."

Chance started down the steps. He descended level after

level, expecting to find a door at any moment. Much to his chagrin, fifteen minutes later he was still descending with no exit in sight. *Should I go back?* He looked up at the stairs he'd descended. They seemed to spiral upward into infinity. *No, I've come too far now. Better to press on.*

He continued his descent. Just when he was reconsidering turning around, he came upon a large, black metal door. "At last! I thought I was never going to get out of here!"

Chance pressed a button on the wall and the door opened to reveal a maze of machinery that stretched on for what seemed like miles. The maze was filled with gigantic black pistons, cylinders, and electrodes buzzing with green energy. *Oh my!* Chance thought as he entered the maze. *It's like I've stepped into Dr. Frankenstein's laboratory!*

A loud crash sounded behind him. He wheeled around and saw that the door through which he'd entered had closed. He pressed buttons on a control panel at its side, trying to get it to open.

"Open!" Chance commanded. Nothing happened. "Open . . . *please.*" The door refused to budge.

He heard a whisper—like the hiss of a snake—behind him. He whirled around but saw nothing but black machinery lit with sickly green light.

"Who's there?" he called. "Show yourself!"

After what seemed like hours, Chance shrugged and proceeded further into the maze. *Maybe I'm going crazy. Maybe my mind is playing tricks—*

"*I sssssee youuuuu!*" a voice hissed.

Chance grabbed a billy club from the holster on his back and spun around. "Come out now! I'm warning you! I'm armed!"

The slight titter of laughter sounded from all around. It was not the fun kind he, Shocker, and S.C. participated in. No, this laughter was malicious and mocking.

Chance wanted to run, but didn't know where to run to. Movement caught the corner of his eye and he spun around. He thought he just saw the edge of something disappear behind a column of machinery.

He jumped behind the massive column, yelling as he brandished his billy club high above his head. Nothing was there. He ran down the nearest pathway, determined to catch his stalker. But the pathway proved devoid of life.

He looked right, left, up, and down. Nothing. "Dang!" Chance was no longer afraid, but frustrated. Then he heard the hiss directly behind him and icy fingers of terror seized his heart.

This is it, he thought. *This is like in all the horrorvids I sneaked out of my room to watch after Mom had gone to bed! This is where the goat-footed demon appears and eats the guy stupid enough to go wandering in the haunted house!*

Chance gulped and spun around to confront the demon.

And there it stood! His heart almost leapt out of his chest. It was different than he'd imagined, but that it was the horror movie demon, he had no doubt. It was enormous, looming over him, milky white and shimmering, fanged and clawed, with cat's eyes. And just like in the movies, Chance knew it was going to kill him.

The specter demon smiled at him, exposing rows of serrated teeth. Then it opened its mouth impossibly wide and lunged at Chance.

Chance ran, scrambling to find safety. He slipped and fell down into a large hole he hadn't noticed before. He struck solid floor several feet down. Dazed, he stood up to find himself in a nearly pitch-black room.

He peered around. He saw something move in the shadows and inhaled in fear. Something was coming out of the dark. Something big.

The something big turned out to be many somethings. All around Chance, ghostly white forms like the specter demon formed out of the shadows. Their faces were contorted with hate. Their arms reached out to squeeze the life from his body.

They moved closer and closer, hissing and shrieking. Terror overcame Chance. His eyes grew wide beneath his mask, threatening to pop right out of his face.

You just had to come to Burlington, didn't you? Chance thought. *Stupid idiot!*

Chance felt something grasp the neck of his suit and he screamed, his horror complete. The end had come.

Then Chance was yanked out of the hole into the dim light. The Dark Thing—the Burlington Board Member who had ripped up his application—loomed large before him. Its red eyes glared down at him from its executioner's hood. "Get hold of yourself," it snapped, disgust in its deep voice.

The Dark Thing turned and dumped Chance on the floor.

It walked toward the specter demon that had scared Chance into falling down the hole. The specter demon raised its claws high in the air, its mouth once again opening to impossible proportions to reveal its rows of fangs.

"No, don't!" Chance watched as The Dark Thing walked right through it, the demon's ghostly form dissipating in smoky wafts as he did so. The Dark Thing turned and looked at Chance.

"They can't hurt you," it said. "They can't do anything anymore." The Dark Thing threw back its cloak and placed its gloved hands on its hips. "I know what you're thinking. But no, they're not ghosts. They're superhuman criminals."

"But it didn't look like a criminal," Chance said. "It looked like a demon—a monster!"

"Are you so dense?" The Dark Thing asked. "Many would say the same about your rocky friend, Block. *Yes, I know all about you two and your teammates.* Surely, by now, you realize superhumans—both heroes and villains—come in all shapes and sizes!"

Chance nodded. Even during his first few days at Burlington, he'd passed countless others on campus who would've defied description in human terms, who looked like monsters.

"But what are supervillains doing roaming beneath the Academy?" Chance asked.

"You truly are thick-headed, aren't you, Fortune?" The Dark Thing sounded exasperated. "Did you not just see me walk through that beast? They're not really here, at all. They exist in the dimensional prison known as The Shadow Zone."

"Shadow Zone?" Chance scrambled to his feet. "Dimensional prison?"

"Yes, The Shadow Zone—a dimensional prison reserved for supervillains too powerful or diabolical to be jailed by conventional means. Now, don't interrupt me again!"

Chance lowered his head.

"An unfortunate side effect of this machinery," The Dark Thing continued, "the machinery that powers Burlington's protective force field—is that its extraneous energy tends to *thin* the dimensional barrier separating us from The Shadow Zone. That's why we can see them and they can see us—at least, down here they can. But like The Shadow Zone's name implies, they are truly no more here in substance than your shadow is."

The Dark Thing swaggered several steps away from Chance, paused as if he'd just remembered something, and then turned. "I've heard all about you and your teammates from Steel Valkyrie," it growled. "But seeing you in person— *you look familiar.* Have we met before? Outside of Burlington, I mean."

Chance gulped. "I, uh, don't think, that, uh, rather, that is, uh—"

The Dark Thing shook its head and then pointed to a door Chance hadn't noticed before.

"Exit's that way. Now get to class!"

Chance craned his head to look at the door. When he turned to thank him, The Dark Thing had disappeared.

Chance exhaled, his entire body relaxing. After a few moments, he headed for the exit.

First, Creeper, then The Shadow Zone, and now The Dark Thing almost recognizes me! Man, I hope nothing else bad happens today!

Later that night, The Imagineer streaked through the sky above the Burlington campus at near light speed, leaving a translucent red photon trail produced by the activation of his crimson hardhat—his power helm—in his wake.

The Imagineer was not only a member of the Burlington faculty and board, but also the appointed Guardian of this space-time realm. It went without saying that his time was precious. So when The Imagineer received an urgent communiqué from Xenoman, he knew big trouble was afoot.

He reached the administration building and willed his helm to loosen the bonds of his molecules as he phased through the wall leading into Xenoman's office.

"Z-man," The Imagineer said as he landed before the large oak desk in his friend's office. "What's the crisis?"

Xenoman rose from behind his desk to stand at his full height of seven feet, his alien frame hidden beneath his shiny green cloak. He towered over The Imagineer.

"I have it on good authority," Xenoman said, "that a hostile alien presence has infiltrated the campus."

"But the Academy's force field is up!" The Imagineer said. "I know. I felt MOTHER's DNA scan when I passed through. How could an alien presence have gotten inside?"

"Oh, there are ways," Xenoman said, coming out from behind his desk to stand before The Imagineer. "No security is foolproof. The Terrormancers taught us that, remember?"

"You're right." The Imagineer shook his head. "Well, what's the plan? Do we know its location?"

"Oh, we know exactly where it is," Xenoman said. "It's right here."

"What? What do you mean, it's right here? What's going on, Z-man?"

Xenoman spread his cloak to reveal the small blond boy clad in the buttoned-up Hawaiian shirt standing before him. The boy was smiling, his face cherubic. But there was something in his eyes. Something far older than the boy appeared to be. Something ancient. Something malevolent.

The boy began unbuttoning his shirt. The Imagineer was not worried. Even if something harmful lay beneath, his helm would automatically throw up a protective field, drawing the power to do so right out of his imagination.

And then he felt it. The bond shared between his mind and the power helm effortlessly severed by Xenoman with a telepathic knife.

"Xenoman," The Imagineer gasped. "What are you do—?"

His words were cut short as tendrils of black pitch sprang from the boy's open shirt to envelop him in utter darkness.

13

The next morning, Chance made it to Dr. Archibald
Claremont's Superhuman History 101 class without incident.
He sat beside Space Cadet in the stadium-style classroom, ab-
sentmindedly fumbling the marbles Jacob had given him
around in his palm. By this time, he'd gotten used to having a
talking gorilla as a professor.

Professor Claremont's superhuman intelligence and powers
of speech had been the unexpected result of testing an experimental drug intended to treat Alzheimer's patients. Decades
ago, the genius ape had used his intellect to fight crime. But
now, in his golden years, the silverback gorilla devoted his
time to his true love—the pursuit of all things academic.

"The Philistine giant known as Goliath," Dr. Claremont
said in his proper British accent, "was hypothesized to have descended from the branch of Nephilm known as the Anakites.
When Joshua took over from Moses, whom we discussed earlier

this week, as leader of the Israelite nation, he conducted a military campaign which exterminated the Anakites from all Middle Eastern territories save for Gaza, Ashdod, and Goliath's homeland of Gath.

"Goliath had issued a vocal challenge to his enemy, the Israelites, calling out their champion to battle one-on-one. Such an *economy-of-warriors* practice was standard in Goliath's time. The *archnemesis rule* occasionally used in our battle team tournaments harkens back to such. But I digress."

Dr. Claremont pushed his spectacles back from the edge of his snout, then continued his lecture.

"Insight into Goliath's immense physical stature and prowess can be gleaned from early Judeo-Christian texts. Goliath was recorded to stand nine feet in height. He was able to move and fight in a coat of armor weighing over sixty pounds. The mere tip of his spear was equal in weight to full-length swords of his day. Goliath's shield was of such enormity that another soldier was assigned the singular duty of bearing it for him onto the battlefield.

"Grant you, these things are not impressive by today's standards, but during Goliath's time he would have been a virtual god among men. Goliath, however, proved to be all too mortal during his people's military campaign against the Israelites."

The hologram of the warrior giant Goliath, which had been rotating before Dr. Claremont, changed into one of a small olive-skinned boy garbed in a tunic and playing a harp while he sat among sheep. Dr. Claremont peered at the new image as he spoke.

"It was not superior force that felled the mighty Goliath,"

he continued, "but rather what, at first glance, would seem to have been a mere boy. A *human* boy, no less. The boy was called David, son of the Ephrathite Jesse of Bethlehem. David was not even a soldier in his nation's army at the time, but rather a simple shepherd. But was there more to this *David* than meets the eye?"

Chance perked up in his seat, considering the professor's words.

"The meaning of his name is our first clue that may, in fact, have been the case. The Hebrew name David actually means *beloved*. According to their own scripture, David was a man after the heart of the Judeo-Christian God, whom they, consequently, would have us believe is the *lord of lords, king of kings, god of gods,* et cetera, et cetera.

"The biblical book of First Samuel recounts David's anointing as the future king of Israel. That a shepherd boy would be chosen as the leader of a nation is odd in and of itself, even in the context of those ancient times. However, chapter sixteen, verse thirteen of that same book reads, in part, that 'from that day on, the Spirit of the Lord came upon David in power.'"

Dr. Claremont paused to wipe the dust from one of the elbow patches of his tweed jacket. Satisfied it was clean, the professor resumed his lecture.

"Taken at face value, this would seem to indicate that a greater force was, in fact, at work in or through young David during his battle with Goliath, and throughout the rest of his life.

"Lending further credence to this theory is the fact that David's legacy would one day produce the first known superhuman ever to return from death to life by means un-aided. But I digress."

Dr. Claremont cleared his throat. "Can young David's victory over the Philistine giant, Goliath, be attributed to a greater power? Most scholars seem to agree that would be the case. The idea of a practically unarmed, unshielded, and super-powerless human boy defeating what was probably the mighti-est warrior of the day without any external aid is absolutely *absurd*."

Chance raised his hand.

"Ah, yes, Mr. Fortune."

"Why?" Chance asked.

"Pardon me?" Dr. Claremont asked. He beat his chest with his fists. It was an unchangeable habit from his youth.

"Not to take away from David's faith," Chance said, "but why is it so hard to believe David defeated Goliath on his own? I know he was just a shepherd boy, but that was no walk in the park back then, was it? I mean, the Bible also records David previously killing at least one bear and one lion, doesn't it?"

Chance scooped up his marbles from the desktop into the palm of his hand. "It's obvious David was extremely brave. Maybe he was also extremely clever. Maybe he saw Goliath, assessed the situation, and then decided what needed to be done. Maybe—maybe David saw he couldn't win under Go-liath's rules, and so he changed the game."

"What rubbish!" a familiar voice said from across the room. "No pimply-faced human smelling of sheep dung could've de-feated one of us by himself!"

Chance turned to see Superion smirking at him while the rest of his teammates laughed and patted the Invincible on his back.

"Bravo, Mr. Fortune," Dr. Claremont said as his ungainly paws did a prim golf clap.

Chance refocused his attention on the professor.

"That," Dr. Claremont said, "is the most interesting—albeit hardly convincing—argument for cheating I've ever had the dubious pleasure of hearing."

The class shouted with laughter.

"Seriously, Mr. Fortune," Dr. Claremont said. "Surely, when looking over the course of David's life, which you seem to be somewhat familiar with, you must agree that, at the very least, he possessed a power of luck equal to your own?"

"Oh," Chance said, "I'd certainly give you that."

"*Indeed.*"

At that moment, the digitized bell signaling class changes sounded and the students began to sprint for the hallway.

"Remember," Dr. Claremont shouted, trying to be heard over the bustle of noise, "your essays on the epic of Gilgamesh are due next Tuesday. No late entries will be accepted!"

Chance exited the classroom with Space Cadet talking his ear off when he noticed Warlock waiting in the hallway. It was obvious the Invincible wanted to talk to him.

What now? Chance thought. He strode past Warlock without speaking, hoping the Invincible would take a hint and leave him alone.

Warlock fell into step beside Chance. "I couldn't help but notice, Fortune, how concerned you were that David might have not defeated Goliath with anything more than—how shall I put this—*human* ingenuity?"

Dang! Chance thought. *I knew I should've kept my big mouth shut! I might as well have had a neon sign hanging over my head in there saying, I'm human! Kick me out of school!*

"Ha!" Chance said, trying to feign indifference. "Just following the tenet of Occam's razor, Warlush—"

"*Warlock*, if you please!"

"Sure, sure, Warlump. Whatever. My point was even the largest of elephants fear the tiniest of mice. There's no reason to add a supermouse into the equation."

Chance looked to S.C. He'd gone silent and was trying to become as unnoticeable as possible.

"Do you come from a superheroing family, Fortune?" Warlock asked. "How, exactly, did you get your superpowers—?"

Better play it cool here, Chance thought. "My records are on file. Just like everyone else's, *Warloser!* Besides, is it a crime to ask questions in class? Or will that get me burned alive—like your big, idiot captain burned Creeper?"

Warlock scowled at Chance. "You'd better watch yourself, Fortune!" His eyes narrowed. "Because I certainly will!" He wheeled around and strode off down another corridor.

Great! Just what I needed. One of Superion's cronies keeping tabs on me!

"Come to think of it, Chance," S.C. said, speaking again now that the coast was clear, "I don't think you've told us how you got your powers." He followed Chance down the hall. "Gothika has an amulet to channel her magic. Psy-chick told us her psionic abilities pass down the female line in her family. Shocker's mother—well, let's just say she was a superhuman groupie. Private Justice happened to be around when one of the DSA's experimental weapons fired. Iron Maiden is the daughter of the Norse god Odin. And I, of course, am the son of two superscientists. What about you—?"

"It's—" Chance struggled to find inspiration. "It's a long story, S.C. Ask me again later. Right now all I can think about is the fact that we have our first team battle today."

"I hear you," Space Cadet said.

Chance gave S.C. a sidelong glance. His teammate seemed satisfied with his answer—he hoped.

Later that afternoon, Chance and his teammates sat in one of Kirby Coliseum's locker rooms trying to come up with a team name while they awaited their first battle.

"How about the Puke Smashers?" Gothika asked. She swept her arm through the air and conjured the words. They glowed for a few moments and then faded. "That's the name of one of my favorite rock bands."

"That's . . . *nice*," Psy-chick said, "but I don't think it's quite what we're all looking for. Good suggestion, though."

"We should call ourselves the Vikings!" Iron Maiden flexed her arms.

"Wow," Gothika said, "that's quite the imagination you have there, Maiden. Never mind the fact that you're the only Viking among us!"

"I like the Revengers!" Private Justice said. He jumped to his feet and thrust a fist in the air. "We could even have a battle cry that tied into it—*Revengers, reassemble!*"

"Are you kidding me?" Shocker scoffed. "That might sound cool—if we were in kindergarten!"

"Well, you come up with a name, then, smarty pants!" Private Justice said.

"'Smarty pants?'" Shocker put his hands over his heart. "P.J., I'm devastated!"

"Don't make fun of him," Psy-chick chided. "Do what he says. If you're so cool, then come up with a team name!"

"I'm an outlaw, princess," Shocker said. "I don't *do* guessing games."

"Wait a second!" Chance said. "That's it!"

"*Bitte?*" Iron Maiden asked.

"Yeah, guys!" Chance rose to his feet. "We're Outlaws!"

"Uh, Chance," Psy-chick said, "I don't care what you did before Burlington—"

"No, no!" Chance said. "Not that kind of Outlaw! The other kind! The good kind! The kind that challenges convention—rebels against the norm!"

"Yeah, cool!" Gothika said. "*The Outlaws.* It's got an edge to it."

"Psy-chick?" Chance asked.

"It beats getting a tattoo to show a little rebellion," she said. "I like it!"

"It's a sad time when the unjust must be counted on to uphold justice," Private Justice said. "But I guess that's why we all put the costumes on in the first place. The Outlaws it is!"

"Yeah, Outlaws!" S.C. cried.

"You know what I think," Shocker said, grinning.

"Iron Maiden—?" Chance asked.

Steel Valkyrie burst into the locker room. "I see you've yet to register your battle team name," she said. "You mean to tell me you had all this time to come up with a team name, *but did not?*"

"Well—ah—we," Iron Maiden fumbled, "you see—"

"The Outlaws," Chance said. "We decided to call ourselves The Outlaws."

"Yeah," Iron Maiden said, relief apparent in her smiling face. "The Outlaws! We're calling ourselves The Outlaws! Of course. Silly me!"

The rest of the team nodded enthusiastically, everyone just as relieved as Iron Maiden to be spared Steel Valkyrie's wrath. Steel Valkyrie surveyed them, one eyebrow raised.

"Not very—becoming," she said. "Especially for a team coached by as prominent a Board Member as myself."

"We are The Outlaws," Iron Maiden said, her eyes hard.

Steel Valkyrie returned her gaze. After a long pause, Steel Valkyrie broke the silence. "Very well. Today, you face Team Manga."

A hologram sprang to life beside her. Team Manga's moniker formed, set against a backdrop of Asian ideograms. The display then changed into VR footage of their battles.

"As you can see, they are a seasoned team of impeccable fighting skill. It is due to that reason that I requested they be our first matchup. No newbie dregs for my—*Outlaws.*" Steel Valkyrie grimaced as if it pained her to say her battle team's name. "Now, please follow me into the Infinity Chamber."

The Outlaws made their way to the inner circle of the Infinity Chamber. Once on the platform, all stood in silence as they awaited Team Manga's arrival. They did not have to wait long.

Technorock music resounded throughout the chamber.

A door on one side of the chamber slid open and out sprang a beautiful young Asian girl, her long, dark hair as black as the skin-tight leather outfit adorning her body. She punched and kicked the air, posing in different martial arts stances.

"Anime!" A deep, loud synthetic voice shouted the name throughout the chamber. Holograms of Asian ideograms and VR recordings of the girl's ICT sessions materialized. Anime leapt into the air, gliding impossible distances without touching the ground. When she reached the Infinity Chamber's inner platform, she somersaulted high into the air and then landed, crouching like a tiger ready to pounce.

Over the music, the voice sounded again.

"Hong Kong Harry!"

An Asian boy in black gloves, trench coat, and sunglasses swaggered out onto the chamber's walk ramp, gnawing on the end of a toothpick. The technorock playing throughout the chamber took on the machine gun riffs of an electric guitar as Harry's personal ideograms and holograms materialized behind him. With a flick of his wrists, Harry threw back the long lapels of his jacket to reveal two pistols hanging in twin shoulder holsters at his sides.

He drew the guns and fired overhead, brass shells ejecting from their chambers as orange fire blazed from their nozzles. Chance saw Space Cadet wince with every shot.

"He can't really *shoot* us, can he?" S.C. whispered to Psychick. She patted his arm reassuringly. "No," she said. "Safety protocols of the battle sessions. The use of lethal force is not allowed."

"But," Private Justice said, "everything just short of that goes. I'll bet whatever bullets he's firing, probably rubber, will leave a heck of a mark!"

S.C. gulped as Hong Kong Harry joined Anime on the platform.

"Tsunami," the synthetic voice boomed. A torrent of rushing water exploded from the chamber entrance, washing down its sides onto the ramp. A second later another Asian girl rode through the entrance on an oceanic wave produced from thin air. She was garbed like an aquatic princess. A thin, ornate crown of coral sat on her head.

"Hubba-hubba!" Shocker said.

Tsunami's theme music, a variation of Hong Kong Harry's—just as his had been a variation of that played for Anime—sounded as her ideograms and holograms formed behind her. She rode the wave the entire length of the ramp. The wave crested and washed over the inner platform's rim as she came to stand beside her teammates.

Shocker lowered his sunglasses, revealing the electric inferno blazing inside him, and gave Tsunami a wink. Tsunami flared her nostrils and crossed her thin arms in response.

"Exo," the voice again boomed.

Both the chamber's entrance door and the ramp widened to allow passage of what appeared to be a van-size robot. The music playing throughout the chamber changed to a metallic version of Tsunami's theme song. Exo consisted of a gigantic torsoless head to which two large apeish robotic arms and two lupine robotic legs were attached.

Upon second glance, Chance saw the egg-shaped torso/head was a cockpit. A boy garbed in a silver helmet and jumpsuit sat inside operating the controls.

Exo lumbered down the ramp and halted beside his teammates.

"Yin and Yang," the voice boomed. Two elaborately dressed Indo-Chinese assassins, a girl clad in blue and a boy clad in yellow, appeared in puffs of smoke. Both of their costumes were equipped with masking veils, swords, cloaks, and golden trim. Their theme music had dual harmonies, which both complemented and contrasted each other. Their holograms formed behind them as they cartwheeled down the ramp, weaving in and out of each other's paths. They reached the inner platform and came to a halt, their cloaks settling around them.

"Dracomon."

Dracomon's theme was a soft, light, happy rendition of those previously played for Team Manga. The Outlaws gave sighs of relief as a small Asian girl peeked out from behind Team Manga's entrance door. Her eyes seemed to smile as she put her hand to her mouth and giggled.

Dracomon walked out onto the ramp. She was dressed in a prep school uniform and wore red barrettes clipped in her silky black hair. Holograms of Dracomon running through fields of wildflowers and butterflies played behind her rather than those of any ICT training sessions.

As she drew closer, Chance saw what looked like a tiny green blob riding on her shoulder. It had hands and feet, but no arms or legs. It also lacked a nose, but a smiling half-moon served as its mouth. Smaller twin half-moons served as its eyes.

Chance noticed the girl wore a necklace. Its pendant was a red tear-shaped stone. Dracomon took her place with her team and smiled and waved at The Outlaws. Much to Steel Valkyrie's obvious displeasure, they waved back. They couldn't resist. She was so cute!

"Robotron," Steel Valkyrie snapped. "If you're quite finished—" Team Manga's theme music stopped playing and silence returned to the Infinity Chamber.

A voice from the empty air beside Steel Valkyrie answered. It sounded as though it was distilled through a digital voice box. "Sorry. All part of the Team Manga aesthetic." There was a flash of light beside Steel Valkyrie and a seven-foot-tall robot samurai appeared.

"Well then," Steel Valkyrie said, "I suppose a coin toss is in order."

"Not so, honorable Valkyrie," Robotron said. "As you have been so gracious in allowing my team this first battle against your team of newbies, I shall yield to you the choice of competition."

Steel Valkyrie did not hesitate. "Last Team Standing."

Robotron gave a digital chuckle. "Are you sure, Lady Valkyrie? Wouldn't you rather engage in something a bit easier for so fresh a team?"

"Last Team Standing," Steel Valkyrie repeated, unyielding. "Choose the terrain."

Robotron gave a metallic sigh. "Very well," he said as he activated the Infinity Posts.

14

When the light show faded, both teams found themselves in the middle of a vast deserted courtyard of a ruined Shaolin temple. Chunks of rubble and debris were strewn all around them. Beyond the courtyard's crumbling walls, Chance saw they were surrounded by large rolling mountains that climbed high into the sky to disappear into the thick gray mist above. Only the presence of the Infinity Posts in the center of the courtyard served as a reminder that they were from a place and time far away.

"All right, men," Private Justice said, his chest swelling as he slapped S.C. on the back. "Today is our day to shine! We must heed the call of battle! We must vanquish our unjust enemy! We must—"

"Shut up!" Shocker said.

"Outlaws," Steel Valkyrie said. "Consider the opening bell

wrung." Both Steel Valkyrie and Robotron tapped their wrist watches and vanished from view.

Rubber bullets and concussion bombs rained down upon The Outlaws from Team Manga's side of the yard, kicking up vast clouds of both dust and dirt. The Outlaws lunged for cover, some leaping behind fallen rubble, others falling prostrate upon the ground, their hands covering their heads. Only Iron Maiden stood her ground.

She stared at Team Manga in defiance as bullets from Hong Kong Harry's guns bounced off her flesh and shock grenades from Exo's cannons exploded around her.

"Charge!" Iron Maiden yelled, then sprinted headlong between the Infinity Posts at Team Manga. She missed her targets. Hong Kong Harry ducked and rolled out of her path and thruster bursts from Exo's legs carried him out of harm's way. But at least the hail of bullets stopped.

From behind his barrier of rubble, Chance spoke into his communicator watch. "Maiden, we should let them come to—" Before he could finish his sentence, the rest of the team came bolting by on either side of him.

Well, Chance thought, *at least we're not cowards.*

"To heck with it!" Chance said and jumped out from behind his hiding place to join his team in battle.

Chance had seen many holorecordings of TCT sessions since arriving at Burlington. They, however, did not even do the slightest bit of justice to the up-close-and-personal, all-out superhuman brawl being fought before his eyes.

Yin and Yang whirled around Private Justice, poking and slicing at him with their swords. Chance saw that the now unsheathed blades were covered with blue and yellow light energy. To P.J.'s credit, he contorted his elastic red and blue body into loops, rings, and holes, expertly dodging their combined onslaught. However, Yin and Yang just as expertly stayed right out of reach of Justice's elongated arms, jumping and flipping nimbly on and over the courtyard debris to avoid P.J.'s assault.

Gothika stood above a crouched Space Cadet, a shield of mystical energy holding a barrage of Exo's laser-guided missiles and rocket-powered smart bombs at bay. She grimaced with the excruciating strain of sustaining the shield against the pounding weaponry.

"Look," Chance heard Shocker say over his communicator watch's open channel. He looked over to see his friend putting the moves on the water princess, Tsunami. "Can't we talk about this peaceably?" Shocker asked. "Maybe improve relations between our two teams?"

Tsunami smiled and leaned forward. She opened her mouth and a surging tide of water crashed outward, blasting Shocker back onto his posterior. He lay there for a moment, blue sparks crawling along his short-circuited body. After some time he recovered and stood up.

"I try to be nice—" Shocker said, scowling as he wrung water from his shirt.

Chance continued his survey of the scene to find Psy-chick engrossed in conflict with Hong Kong Harry. Harry ran and jumped, leapt and turned, firing his weapons at Psy-chick from every possible angle, position, and stance only to have her telekinetically freeze the bullets in the air. Psy-chick allowed a substantial group of them to gather and then sent the bullets zipping back at Harry. With amazing agility, Harry flipped and dodged out of their respective paths.

This isn't the way to go about this, Chance thought. *We should be acting as a team, not this collective of individuals.* His thoughts were cut short as the wind whooshed out of his lungs and he found himself sprawled upon the ground.

"It is not wise," a girl's voice said, "to daydream while engaged in battle."

Chance looked up to see the leather-clad Anime standing over him in a fighting stance, one hand held high behind her head like a fencer, the other outstretched, palm up. She smiled and gestured for Chance to get up. He did not have to be asked twice.

Chance kicked out his legs, springing up from the ground to land on his feet and take a jab at Anime all in one single, smooth motion. She deflected his blow, countering with her forearm. However, Chance was not deterred in the slightest, and advanced upon Anime with a torrent of jabs, swings, punches, kicks, and strikes.

Anime countered his every move, matching Chance blow for blow as if she knew what attack he would throw at her before he did. They continued with their ballet of violence for the length of the courtyard, their forearms winding in and around each other's, their shins and elbows banging and blocking attacks, Chance driving her ever backward.

As their combat drew them closer to the temple itself,

Chance realized he was working up a sweat and enjoying himself in the process. His ICT sessions were all well and good, but his synthetic opponents had thus far lacked the unpredictability and sheer rawness of true physical combat.

I haven't had a workout like this since I sparred against Lei Chan's grandson, Chance thought, recalling the time Captain Fearless's old friend from China had visited Littleton.

Chance kicked and punched his way with Anime across the courtyard until her back came within inches of the decrepit wall sectioning off the ruins from the outside terrain. He brought up his hand to strike Anime. She seized his forearm, halting the blow just as it was about to strike her on the temple. They froze in that position for a moment, the sound of Chance's rapid breathing interrupting the otherwise complete silence.

Chance was distressed to see that Anime wasn't breathing hard in the slightest. But she was smiling. A feeling of dread rose within his gut as it dawned upon him that Anime hadn't attempted to strike him since her first blow. She had merely blocked and retreated as he attacked and advanced.

"Not bad," Anime said, "but not good enough!"

Her right hand knifed toward Chance's eyes. He brought up his left arm just in time to deflect her blow. It merely glanced off his temple. Then Anime's left hand came up, then her left foot, then her right, over and over again. Chance found himself struggling to defend against Anime's attack. Now it was he who retreated, stepping back and back and back.

"Get off my leg, you toad!" Gothika screamed at Space Cadet. "This is hard enough as it is!"

"Sorry." S.C. released his hold around Gothika's right leg as though he'd been burned by a hot iron. A missile from Exo's armor launched itself at the two Outlaws. Gothika threw up her hand and the projectile broke apart and flew away from them as it transformed into a swarm of moths. S.C. gasped in surprise and accidentally swallowed one. His face turned green and he began to gag.

"Can't you do something?" Gothika asked, her tone desperate, orange sparks leaping from her fingertips to cascade harmlessly over Exo's shell. S.C. thought for a moment.

"I need something to work with," he said as lasers from Exo's gun turrets bore down on Gothika's protective magical shield. "Something mechanical. Can you get me one of his arms?"

"Fat chance of that happening," she said. "What do you want me to do? Waltz over there and ask him if he'll play nice while I magically cut off his arm?"

"Well," S.C. said, "his hand then. A finger! Anything!"

Gothika mumbled something under her breath. S.C. thought it could have been incantations, curses, or both. Exo drew closer and closer to them, his lasers gaining intensity with every step his lumbering armor took toward them.

Then S.C. saw something sprout from the ground around the robotic vehicle's foot. He watched as the something, now a tangle of small vines, wove its way around Exo's metal foot. Space Cadet looked up at Gothika. Sweat poured down her grimacing face. It was obvious the extra amount of willpower and concentration the dual spells were taking was staggering. S.C. felt helpless.

Exo tried to lift his foot to continue his advance but faltered. The vines now tugged at his right leg. The robot yanked and jerked, attempting to free itself while redoubling its attack upon Gothika's magical defenses. The vines stretched and stretched but it was Exo's mechanized foot that gave way. It remained within the tangled web of roots while the robotic body continued forward.

At that moment, Exo's lasers penetrated Gothika's weakened magical energy shield to find their mark. The beams blasted her backward.

"Gothika!" S.C. shouted as he watched her land. She was unconscious. He heard the clank of Exo's legs and watched as a giant black shadow covered him. S.C. gulped with fear and turned to face the inevitable.

"There's no escape from Justice!" Private Justice called as his elongated arms just missed putting Yin in a vise-like grip. He was finally making headway! Yin and Yang had given up any sort of offensive attack. They now merely retreated, the desire to battle seemingly worn out of them.

If the spirit's defeated, P.J. thought, *the body will soon follow!*

Yin and Yang stood side by side before Justice, all but daring him to grab them.

I know their game. They'll split up at the last second. Well, try as you might, my two-tone friends, Justice will have his day!

Private Justice went for them, his arms and body stretching both long and far. The two assassins split up, running in opposite directions. P.J. would not so easily be undone. He sent an arm snaking along after each of them.

P.J. was so caught up in apprehending his two opponents he did not notice when they circled back toward each other behind a set of crumbling statues. Out of his sight, he felt his arms grasp hold of something and then close tight. P.J. realized he had his men. "Justice is served!" he proclaimed.

A moment later, Private Justice was shocked to see both Yin and her yellow-clad counterpart, Yang, step out from behind the statues, free of bondage.

"What the—?" P.J. tried to retract his arms but found they would not return. He flexed again and again, the spongy bones, cartilage, and muscle seeking to shrink, but to no avail. They must have tied his arms together!

"Hey!" P.J. yelped as he felt his legs being yanked out from under him. He'd been so concerned with his arms he'd failed to notice Yin and Yang running toward him. They took hold of his legs. Yin ran with one until she came to a boulder resting in the temple courtyard. She rounded the rock several times and then tied the appendage to it. Yang did the same with P.J.'s other leg. Their jobs done, the pair walked over to stare down at Justice.

"You'll never get away with this," P.J. said. "Justice will prevail!"

The pair laughed as they unsheathed their blue and yellow energy blades.

Shocker brought down his arms with a hard yank, criss-crossing his wrists. A large bolt of blue electricity exploded outward from the tips of his fingers. Tsunami's body shimmered into liquid form and then split apart like the Red Sea divided. "Oh, flarn. I missed!"

The water re-formed itself into Tsunami's whole body and then shot out from her fingertips in liquid blasts. Shocker stretched his arms out at his sides. Blue sparks covered his entire body, creating a protective electrical web. The water struck the energy field and evaporated into steam.

Then Shocker let loose another bolt of electricity from his right hand, this one aimed at the water surrounding Tsunami's feet. *Surely this will get her,* he thought. Sure enough, Tsunami disappeared from view. All that was left of her were a few clouds of rising steam.

Got her! He rushed over to the area where his foe had been standing, hoping she would soon re-form so he could gloat over his victory.

A few seconds went by, but no Tsunami. *Oh no! I didn't mean to—!* But before he could finish his thought, Shocker noticed a damp spot on the ground enlarging as if it were seeping up from the earth. *What the—?*

Shocker's question was answered as a geyser exploded from the ground at his feet. It carried him high into the air and tossed him hard upon the courtyard.

Shocker lay upon the ground for the second time in his

battle with the water princess, fighting seizures as blue sparks rode the length of his body. He looked up to see the geyser bearing Tsunami's cold eyes and smile. A large crumbling statue rode high on its crest, ready to be dashed down upon him at any moment.

Psy-chick grimaced in deep concentration. *If only I could telekinetically pull the guns from Hong Kong Harry's hands,* she thought, *or get inside his mind.* But she could do neither. It was all she could do to keep the continual hail of bullets at bay. They had not been able to penetrate her telekinetic shield. The projectiles hung before her in the air, countless more joining the barrage every second.

Harry fired on and on and on, never needing to reload. Psy-chick wondered if that was part of his power—to pull matter from some pocket dimension and convert it into a continual stream of bullets for his guns. *Keep your mind on the job at hand, girl!* Psy-chick thought. *Just the smallest slip in concentration and—Hey, what's he doing?*

Psy-chick saw Harry take aim elsewhere with one of his pistols for just the briefest of moments as he fired a single shot. She realized only too late that Harry had made a ricocheting shot. The rubber bullet glanced off the statue behind her and then glanced off her back, knocking her to the ground.

A shadow loomed over Psy-chick. She looked up to see the toothpick wiggling in an excited dance between Hong Kong Harry's smiling teeth as he again took aim.

"What a cute little pet," Iron Maiden said as she bent down and tickled the smiling blob of green on the girl's shoulder. It giggled at her touch. "What do you call it, Dracomon?"

The girl smiled back at Iron Maiden, her face wide and innocent above her school uniform. "Oh I'm not Dracomon," the girl said. "My name is Chihiro." She turned her head to peer down at the little green blob on her shoulder. "*He's* Dracomon."

The little happy blob smiled and then belched a humongous torrent of flame. The blast enveloped Maiden. When the flames receded, Iron Maiden was left standing with her eyes wide with surprise. A layer of black soot covered her entire body, and her luxuriant auburn braid was now frizzed into a sooty Afro.

Chihiro grasped the tear-shaped pendant hanging about her neck and closed her eyes, her expression serene. Iron Maiden watched in disbelief as the little blob riding on the girl's shoulder grew and grew, hard jade scales forming over its gelatinous hide, horns sprouting from its head and brow, whiskers and razor-sharp teeth budding from its snout. Moments later, Dracomon had revealed himself to be a gigantic Oriental dragon, his snakelike body rising from behind Chihiro to tower hundreds of feet above both her and Maiden. Dracomon eyed Iron Maiden hungrily, the waterfall of drool from his mouth cascading down to melt the statues and rubble upon which it fell.

"Oh, *scheisse!*" Iron Maiden said.

15

Battered and bloodied, Chance tried with ever-increasing desperation to deflect Anime's blows. Unlike Anime, Chance hadn't been able to land a single punch. *This is hopeless. I've got to buy myself some time and regroup.* Chance's thoughts were cut short when he found his body frozen in time and space. He was half-aware that the same fate hadn't befallen Anime; if anything, her body seemed to be moving at miraculous speed as she rose into the air and sent a foot flying into his chest.

The pain of the blow catapulted Chance back into reality. Time and space flowed once more as his body sailed backward through the air until he crash-landed into a pile of rubble. *How the heck did she do that?* Chance wondered as he lay there gasping for breath.

He raised his head to see Anime place her open hands palm-to-palm and draw them back to her side as she waited in a fighting stance. Chance's eyes widened as he saw energy spark and then grow into a fiery, glowing ball at the space where her palms touched.

He rolled out of the way just as Anime extended her arms, thrusting her hands forward, the energy ball rocketing out of her grip to explode in the very spot where Chance had been lying mere nanoseconds before.

"And I actually *wanted* to come to this school!" Chance moaned. He leapt behind a pile of rubble as another energy blast exploded. *Who am I kidding? I don't belong here. I never did. I'm way out of my league. What an idiot I was to think I could hang with superhumans! Stupid! Stupid!*

Chance looked around to see his teammates in even worse shape than himself. Yin and Yang were poised to turn Justice into mincemeat. S.C. and Gothika were about to be blown up and then trampled by Exo. Shocker was in his usual position where girls were concerned, down and out.

And Iron Maiden was getting flung around like a rag doll by a full-fledged fire-breathing dragon! *Holy schnikees!*

Worst of all, Psy-chick was about to become Swiss cheese.

She needed him!

His team needed him.

Chance scanned the courtyard, his team, the temple, desperately seeking some slight advantage, something he'd previously overlooked. Then he saw it.

Anime rose into the air above his shelter, hanging frozen in the sky in a crane stance, her high-pitched battle cry ringing through the air, the horizon behind her changed into a corona of speed lines. Then she dived like a hawk about to snatch a rabbit out of hiding. Chance raised his arm above his head, his grappling gun held tight within his fist. Its line shot forth and then reeled him out of harm's way at the last second as Anime brought her boot down upon empty ground.

Anime leapt after Chance, the arch of her jump taking her over an impossible length of ground. Chance evaded her once more, firing his cable cord high into the air. It struck home between two scales at Dracomon's neck. He hit his grappling gun's reel button and shot upward toward Dracomon and his menacing fanged jaws.

Iron Maiden stood inside the cave of Dracomon's mouth, trying to keep its jagged teeth from clamping down around her. The heat issuing from the monster's throat was unbearable even with her nearly invulnerable skin. Dracomon's saliva scorched her clothes and armor. Iron Maiden heard Chihiro giggling from her perch at the base of Dracomon's skull. It was now Chihiro who rode on her pet's shoulders.

Suddenly, Chihiro's giggles changed into an exasperated sigh. The next thing Iron Maiden knew she was hurtling through the air, spewed out from the dragon's mouth.

Chance landed on Dracomon's scaly hide, grabbing a handhold with one arm while holstering his grappling gun with the other. He looked up and saw his target only a few yards ahead. He heard a thump, or rather felt it through the sensitive dragon scales and looked behind him to see Anime land a football field length down below him. She began closing the distance, leaping several rows of giant scales at a time, the laws of physics bending for her. Chance got moving.

He scrambled upward, clambering over the rough terrain until he reached his goal. Chihiro did not notice his proximity. She sat on her monster's head giggling, her eyes rolled up within her head as if she were in a trance. Chance paid this only a second's notice. He snatched his objective, the teardrop-shaped pendant hanging from around her neck. Chihiro shrieked, her pupils widening as she reached for her absent pendant.

Chance paid this no attention. He leapt off Dracomon's head, Anime in close pursuit.

"Don't blame yourself," Hong Kong Harry said. "You were up against Hong Kong Harry—the best there is!" He peered down at Psy-chick, his face the picture of smugness. "Surrender now and I'll spare y—"

The next second, Hong Kong Harry was laid out on the ground by Chance's boots. Chance tossed Psy-chick Chihiro's pendant and then took off. Psy-chick stepped backward just in time to dodge Anime as she came sprinting by her.

Psy-chick!

Chance? Psy-chick thought, uncertain if she'd actually heard Chance's thoughts inside her mind. She knew whatever he was thinking must be important if he was loosening the shield around his mind so that they could trade thoughts.

Yes, it's me, Chance thought. *You have that pendant?*

Yeah—?

Good! I need your help!

Space Cadet saw that Exo's pilot was grinning ear-to-ear through the robotcraft's windshield.

"Pathetic—coward—no honor," Exo said, his voice toneless as translated through the digital speakers mounted along the armor's body. "I will first let you watch while I finish off your partner, then return for you."

The robotcraft stepped over S.C.'s quivering body and limped on toward Gothika.

Got to work fast! S.C. thought as he scrambled toward the mechanical foot entangled within Gothika's vines. He reached the robotic appendage and tugged, but the foot held in its trap. S.C. looked over his shoulder to see Exo closing in on Gothika. She was conscious, but too weak to do anything more than watch as the huge robot and its pilot advanced upon her.

S.C. pulled and pulled, straining with the effort. The foot ripped free and came up in his hands to smack him in the forehead. He massaged his forehead and set to work.

Such a small thing for such an enormous obstacle, he thought. *I have to make it work, though! I have to!*

Space Cadet's hands raced to dismantle the foot. He whispered nonsensical litanies under his breath, sweat beading his forehead as he struggled to assemble whatever contraption his imagination and skill could muster. He glanced over his shoulder to see Exo standing over Gothika, multiple targeting lasers dotting her body. S.C. snapped the final piece of his construct in place and then turned to face his opponent.

"Hey!" S.C. called. "Exo!"

The robot and its pilot wheeled around to face him, guns cocking, missiles locking onto S.C.'s round purple form. S.C. stood there trembling, the mechanical foot now a tiny pistol in his shaking hands.

"Ah," Exo said, its voice toneless and digitized. "What's this? The mouse come out of its hole to face the tiger? And with such a pitiful little weapon, too. Well, go ahead, mouse. Give it your best shot."

S.C. closed his eyes, turned his head away, and fired. There was a slight spark from the pistol's nozzle, then a puff of smoke, and then nothing. Exo laughed, its voice eerie and emotionless, and stepped toward S.C., its large metal feet leaving tracks in the ground three inches deep. S.C. looked down at the toe gun and beat at it with his fist. Exo drew closer and closer, his synthetic laugh growing louder and louder.

Space Cadet hit the gun again and was propelled backward as a gigantic energy blast exploded outward from the tiny pistol to encompass the robotcraft in an enormous wave of crackling green light.

The wave dissipated to leave Exo's pilot hanging in midair, the robot armor around him disintegrated in its entirety. No longer masked by his exosuit's speakers, the pilot's laugh was revealed to be high and shrill. The laughter stopped as the pilot's posterior hit the ground with a loud thud. He sat there a moment. Then he fainted.

Yin and Yang raised their blue and yellow energy blades high above their heads, their brows furrowing through the eye slits of their costumes. They brought their arms downward with blinding speed, intent upon finishing off Private Justice. Suddenly, their swords disappeared!

Yin and Yang spun around to find a sooty, stinky Iron Maiden standing behind them, her long braid burned into an Afro. She held their swords in her hands. Iron Maiden clenched her fists and the swords shattered.

"I—" Maiden said, "am *not*—happy!"

Yin and Yang stood before her, dumbfounded. Iron Maiden brought down her hands and thumped her opponents' chests with a single finger. Yin and Yang flew through the air and landed unconscious several yards off in the distance.

The giant angry geyser that was Tsunami towered over Shocker, ready to dash the statue spinning at its top down upon him.

"Last chance," Shocker said as he winced in pain. "Give up now—and I'll—take it—easy on you."

Tsunami's watery face grew even more enraged. Her geyser body contracted and then expanded, tossing the statue high into the air. Shocker watched as it plummeted toward him.

Well, Shocker thought, *it was fun while it lasted.* Then his field of vision was covered by a blanket of blue and red.

Private Justice expanded over Shocker's body, encasing him in a large rubbery bubble. The statue hit, its bulk sagging down deep into P.J.'s form and then bounced out to crash onto the courtyard and break apart.

"*Eci! Eci! Ybab! Oot dloc! Oot dloc,*" Gothika chanted, her hands stretched out before her toward Tsunami. Tsunami's rushing geyser form froze into a massive, immobile block of ice.

P.J. retracted his body to its normal lanky proportions and then helped a staggering Shocker to his feet.

"I was—just about—to let her—have it."

Chance hit the ground running as he landed at the far side of the courtyard. He sprinted the remaining length until he found himself inches from a section of temple wall far too high for him to jump and far too smooth to climb. He turned to see Anime striding across the courtyard, her leaps and bounds as smooth and graceful as any African gazelle. She closed the distance between them within seconds.

"All out of things to swing from," Anime said, gloating. "Nowhere left to run." She put her hands together and drew them back to her side, the fiery energy ball forming between her curved fingers. "Too bad. I bet you're cute beneath that mask."

Just as she was about to strike, Anime was mashed to the ground, knocked unconscious by and imprisoned beneath the massive clawed foot of Dracomon. Several hundred feet in the air above, Chihiro bawled as she beat her fists against the back of her disobedient monster's head.

Across the courtyard, Psy-chick released her hold upon Chihiro's teardrop pendant and the monster it controlled.

"Weeeeeee, are the champions, my friends!" Space Cadet sang loudly, off key.

After their battle with Team Manga, The Outlaws had convened in one of McFarlane Cafeteria's anterooms for a victory party of pizza, soft drinks, and potato chips. Chance let the room's soda machine scan his thumb. A second later, the machine dispensed a canned drink. He popped open its tab and collapsed into a hoverchair. He was exhausted from the battle.

"That's great, Pud," Shocker said. "But don't get too cocky. That's *my* job!"

"Oh, come on," Psy-chick said. "Didn't we get enough of that from Steel Valkyrie?

"Yeah, could you believe her?" Gothika placed her can on a hovertable and then mimicked Steel Valkyrie's posture, sucking in her belly and sticking out her chest to ridiculous limits.

"Now, students," she said, doing a very good impression of Steel Valkyrie's condescending tone and facial expressions. "You were lucky today. But don't let it go to your heads! Despite your victory, you may very well be the sorriest battle team I've ever had the burden to instruct."

Save for P.J. and Iron Maiden, the group chuckled.

"You shouldn't make fun of Steel Valkyrie," Private Justice

said. "She's one of Burlington's best battle instructors. She knows what she's doing."

"Does she?" Iron Maiden asked in a bleak tone. The group fell silent. She'd washed most of the soot from her body, but her hair still refused to be tamed. Up until now, she hadn't uttered a single word since they'd warped back into the coliseum. "She chose the wrong team captain, after all."

She got to her feet. "Chance."

He was sitting with his head down, staring at his soft drink can.

"Chance," Iron Maiden repeated.

Chance looked up and met Iron Maiden's gaze. "Hmmmm?"

"I want you to take over as team captain."

"What?" he asked, flabbergasted. "Me? Why? You're doing fine. We won out there today!"

"Yes," Iron Maiden said, "we did. Thanks to your quick thinking. And not for the first time, either."

"But, Maiden," Chance said, "I got lucky. I'm no leader. I—"

"That's not true, and you know it!"

The Outlaws eyed one another in unspoken agreement.

"Chance, Steel Valkyrie appointed me team captain because I'm the most powerful among us. Well, that and—" Iron Maiden paused as if she were choking on her words, "because she's my—my mother."

The Outlaws stared at her in disbelief.

Chance thought about how Steel Valkyrie had been especially hard on Iron Maiden during their practice sessions, never uttering a single word of praise in her direction, setting such a higher standard for her than the rest of them, always pushing and pushing and pushing. His heart went out to her.

"Why—why didn't you tell us?" Gothika asked.

Iron Maiden shrugged. "Just once, it would've been nice to be my own person, rather than 'Steel Valkyrie's daughter.' People always expect me to be just like her. They expect me to be just as—*perfect*."

"You're close enough to perfect for me, Red," Shocker said.

"Shocker, please. Enough," Iron Maiden said. But she had a slight grin on her face as she continued. "I never wanted to be team captain. Mother thinks just because I'm the strongest, I should be the leader. But that's ridiculous! I—I realize that now."

She crossed the room and took a seat beside Chance. "But you *are* a leader. And a wise one, too. We've all seen it every day in our TCT sessions. Somehow you always get us working together. And you do it without even trying.

"I am a warrior," she continued. "A fighter! Don't worry me with logistics and strategy! Just point me in a direction and let me go!"

Iron Maiden placed a hand on Chance's shoulder. "You owe this to yourself," she said. "You owe it to *us*."

The rest of the team yelled and whistled, urging Chance to take up his rightful role. Chance stared down at his soft drink, mulling things over in his mind. He couldn't lie to himself. This was exactly why he'd defied logic, reason, *and law* to come to Burlington in the first place. He wanted this more than anything.

He looked up at Iron Maiden and spoke loud enough so everyone heard him.

"Iron Maiden," Chance said, "when the rest of us ran scared today, you stood and faced Team Manga like a true warrior born. You are a great and brave fighter, and you should have nothing but pride in your heart about that."

He turned and faced the rest of his teammates.

"Okay," he said, grinning. "You talked me into it."

Cheers of jubilation rang throughout the room.

16

Having Psy-chick serve as a mental communications link between the team was the first change Chance made when he accepted the position of team captain. By abolishing watch-radio communication, he could direct The Outlaws to act with the complete secrecy and speed of thought. The other battle teams had quickly caught on to the obvious benefits of this initiative. Those with telepaths strong enough had followed suit—and those were the teams victorious in battle. In effect, Chance had all but revolutionized the way battles were fought at the Academy.

As August and September rolled by, The Outlaws became known as the team to watch. Steel Valkyrie had objected to the change of leadership at first. But victory after victory quickly made a believer out of her. Once she began to win acclaim for instructing such a successful young team, she started fawning over Chance as if he were her own child, much to his dismay.

"If only you could have done so well!" she constantly said to Iron Maiden. To her credit, Iron Maiden took her mother's remarks in stride.

As they were a freshman team without a single loss during their first two months of competition, comparisons between The Outlaws and The Invincibles now ran rampant across campus. This was not lost on Superion and his Invincibles. Holograms reading "The Out-losers stink!" and "Fat Chance Fortune" began to mysteriously crop up all over campus.

"Not again!" Chance said as he, Shocker, and Psy-chick happened upon the latest prank at their expense, a hologram projected on the side of Lee Old Main that read "Private Justice or Private Joke?"

"That's nothing," Psy-chick said. "Gothika's still trying to come up with a spell to remove that green gunk Delilah slipped into her shampoo bottle!"

"I'm sick of this junk!" Shocker raised his hand and a bolt of electricity leapt from it to fry the holoprojector's circuitry. The hologram disappeared.

"Truth hurts, doesn't it?" a familiar voice said.

Chance and his friends looked up to see Superion standing in front of them, a self-satisfied smile on his face. The wererat Ratticus stood hunched over beside him, giggling as he twitched his whiskers.

"Truth hurth!" Ratticus repeated, lisping through his two front incisors.

"The truth is you're a todak!" Shocker yelled at Superion.

"Temper, temper," Superion said, waving his finger in Shocker's face.

"Yeth, temper, temper!" Ratticus repeated.

"I've had enough of you, Francis!" Shocker said.

Superion's eyebrows raised in fury. Ratticus gasped and froze beside him, wringing his clawed hands.

"What did you call me?" Superion asked.

"You heard me, Francis!" Shocker grinned. "Oh, yeah. We got the whole lowdown on you from Block. I think your real name is sooo sweet!"

"Shut up!" Superion said. "Nobody calls me that!"

"Sure thing, Francis!" Shocker said, "I'll never mention it again, Francis!"

"Why you—!" Superion's eyes turned red.

At that moment, everyone froze and looked up to see Alpha-Man streaking across the sky. "You're lucky we're in public," Superion said once Alpha-Man had passed over them. "Come to the party tonight, Shocker. I'll save you a *dance!*"

Superion swiveled on his heels and stomped off. "Come on, Ratticus!" The wererat turned and scampered after his team captain.

"I just bet you will, Francis!" Shocker shouted after them.

"You better be careful," Psy-chick said.

"We're not scared of that todak!" Shocker said. "Right, Hicksville?"

"Of course not," Chance said. "But Psy-chick's right. It's only smart to err on the side of caution where Superion is concerned."

"He's all talk!" Shocker said.

"So are you," Chance said. They all grinned at one another.

"Tough crowd," Shocker said. "Well, I got to split. Tell Iron Maiden I'll collect that dance she owes me tonight."

"You cheated, Shocker," Psy-chick said. "That coin had heads on both sides."

"Hey," Shocker said, raising his arms as he walked backward and away from them. "You can't blame me if she didn't inspect the coin we were flipping. Big Red lost that bet fair and square!"

"He's a mess," Psy-chick said as they watched Shocker go.

"He's that, all right," Chance said.

"So," Psy-chick said as they exited the coliseum, "what are you going as tonight?" It was Halloween and the annual Burlington Academy Costume Party was being held that night in the cafeteria.

"It's a surprise," Chance said.

"Oh, I do like surprises," Psy-chick said.

"Then get ready for a granddaddy of one," Chance said.

They exchanged smiles and then headed toward their dorm rooms.

Two hours later, Chance looked in his holomirror to see a wolfboy worthy of Lon Chaney Jr. staring back at him. He marveled to see that when he furrowed his brow, the wolfboy also furrowed his. When Chance snarled and bared his teeth, the wolfboy did likewise with his snout and fangs.

Perfect, Chance thought. *Just like in the old Universal flicks.*

Now for the final touches. He picked up the tattered breeches and shredded shirt from the floor and placed them over the synthetic mats of fur now covering his body. His clothes appeared stretched and torn as if ripped apart during his transformation into a nightmarish man-beast. *Psy-chick is going to absolutely freak!* Chance thought, pleased with his costume.

Whistling, he left his room, rode the lift plank down to the bottom floor, and exited the dorm. It was now night, and a storm raged down upon Megalopolis. Chance looked up to see torrents of rain hammering soundlessly upon Burlington's dome-shaped force field.

The yard outside Buscema was deserted except for several piles of accumulating debris. Chance had noticed similar piles of trash cropping up in corners and under hovertables all around campus lately. *Someone needs to kick the maintenance drones into high gear!*

Chance was pleased no one was around to see his costume. He hoped to make it to the party before unveiling himself. He was confident his extra efforts would bring him first place in the costume contest. He imagined going up on the hoverstage before the crowd, Psy-chick applauding the loudest as he accepted a large golden trophy and its adorning blue ribbon.

He reached the cafeteria and walked through McFarlane's entrance. When he got inside, Chance's jaw dropped. Everywhere he looked there were people dressed in suits and ties, dresses and skirts, jeans and button-ups, shorts and T-shirts, baseball caps and pocketbooks. They sipped punch and chatted while a DJ played music beside a portion of floor sectioned off for dancing.

"Chance?"

Chance turned to face the hoarse voice addressing him. It belonged to a large male wolf walking upright upon its hind legs. Unlike Chance's costume, the wolf's muzzle and teeth were real.

"Nightwolf? Is that you?" Chance asked. The lab coat, glasses, and stethoscope the werewolf was wearing made the Outlaw uncertain.

"Yeah. I thought that was you," Nightwolf said. "Uh—great—costume."

"Thanks," Chance said. Then he mumbled under his breath, "I guess."

"You're welcome," Nightwolf said. "What do you think of mine? I'm a *doctor*." He pronounced the word *doctor* as if it were some awe-inspiring extraterrestrial entity.

"It's great," Chance said, wondering if he should tell him he probably shouldn't wear his stethoscope like a headband.

"Thanks," Nightwolf said, pleased. Then he changed the subject. "I watched your battle against the Screaming Mercenaries today. You guys sure shellacked them!"

"Yeah." Chance sighed.

"Well, good seeing you." Nightwolf wandered off into the crowd.

"So much for winning the costume contest," Chance mumbled. "What an idiot! I should've realized—Halloween *would* be the one night for people who go in costume year-round to actually dress like normal folks. Sheesh!" He made his way through the crowd, ignoring the snickers directed at him, and joined Space Cadet, Shocker, and Private Justice at the refreshment counter.

"Go ahead," Chance said. "Get it out of your system, Shocker."

Shocker, in his usual attire of leather jacket, sunglasses, and bandanna, doubled over and guffawed.

"Definitely not regulation attire," P.J. said. Private Justice was dressed in a three-piece suit, glasses, and a chain watch.

"I think it's cool, Chance," S.C. said. He was dressed in a snug-fitting African safari outfit complete with tan shorts, button-up shirt, boots, and hat.

"Oh my!" Psy-chick walked toward them trying to stifle a laugh as she stared at Chance. She was dressed in an evening gown.

"Et tu, Brute?" Chance asked.

"Ha! Nice reference," Psy-chick said. "There's nothing a girl likes more than a guy who knows his Shakespeare." She held out her hand. "What you need is a dance to cheer you up."

"I don't much feel like—"

"Please?"

Chance sighed, stood up, and let Psy-chick lead him onto the dance floor.

"Speaking of dances," Shocker said as he watched Chance and Psy-chick on the dance floor, "anyone seen Red?"

"Maybe she stayed in the dorms with Gothika," P.J. said.

"Gothika's not coming?" S.C. asked.

"Before today's battle," Private Justice said, "I overheard her telling Psy-chick that she 'doesn't *do* dances.'"

"Yeah, yeah," Shocker said. "But keep your eye out for Iron Maiden. She owes me—oh, wait. There she is!"

Shocker spotted Iron Maiden beckoning to him from across the room. "Don't wait up for me, boys!" He pushed through the crowd of dancing students toward her. She gestured for him to follow her through an open doorway on the other side of the cafeteria. Iron Maiden slipped inside the doorway and disappeared from view.

Shocker smiled and renewed his chase. He bolted through the open door. He found Iron Maiden among the shadows on its other side waiting for him, a smile on her face. He was reaching for her when the lights came on and Shocker found himself surrounded by The Invincibles.

"Thank you, Delilah," Superion said. "You may leave now."

Shocker gasped as Iron Maiden transformed into The Invincibles's sole female member, Delilah.

"Tough break, lover boy!" Delilah exited the room, passing the black-clad Raz as he entered. Raz closed the door behind her.

Shocker raised his hands to blast Superion. Thanks to Raz's powers of negation, nothing happened. Ratticus and Speed Demon grasped Shocker by his arms in order to restrain him.

"MOTHER!" Shocker cried.

"Oh," Superion said, popping his knuckles, "I'm afraid MOTHER can't hear or help you at the moment. You see, my friend Raz here is powerful enough that he negates even her exceptional sensory registers at areas of low concentration, such as this otherwise insignificant anteroom."

Shocker turned to look into Raz's glossy dead eyes as he felt the negator's cold hand upon his shoulder. He heard dance music booming on the door's other side and knew MOTHER was not the only one unable to hear him.

"I told you I'd save you a dance," Superion snarled. "Lights out, electric boy!"

Chance and Psy-chick danced to the techno music thumping all around them. Psy-chick moved gracefully in time to the beat while Chance stumbled over his own feet. *Give me a good battle-room brawl over this any day,* he thought.

The music slowed to a waltz. Chance saw the couples all around them embrace for a slow dance. He looked back at Psy-chick to see her staring at him expectantly. *Where angels fear to tread,* Chance thought.

He stepped forward and placed his hands on her sides. Her arms went up to his shoulders. They rocked back and forth in an awkward motion, a foot of empty space between them.

"So," Chance said, "you did great out there today against the Screaming Mercenaries."

"Is battle competition all you ever think about?" Psy-chick asked.

"Well, ah," Chance said, "er, uh, well, no. I mean, I think about other things!"

"Like what?" Psy-chick asked. She gently touched his forehead with her index finger. "That mind of yours is a big mystery to me, after all. You continue to keep your thoughts sealed up tight."

She smiled mischievously. "So tight, in fact, one might think you had something to hide."

Chance froze in step so quickly Psy-chick's momentum sent her crashing into him. "Well," she said, "I see I've hit a nerve!"

Chance tried to think of something to say, but he couldn't concentrate. Psy-chick's words had caught him completely off guard. And her nearness—her touch, her smell—wouldn't let him focus on anything but her.

And deep down, he wanted to tell her. Deep down, he wanted Psy-chick to know everything.

"Psy-chick, I—"

"Oh no!" Psy-chick cried, staring over his shoulder, eyes wide.

Chance whirled around to see Shocker crawling across the cafeteria floor. He was severely beaten, blood and bruises covering his face. The crowd parted for him but was too shocked to do anything.

Chance and Psy-chick ran to him. Chance reached Shocker first, sliding down onto his knees and then taking his friend in his arms. Seconds later, the rest of The Outlaws joined them.

"I don't—feel—so good," Shocker said and then fainted.

"MOTHER," Chance yelled. "We need a nurse! Now!"

"Stop the music!" Steel Valkyrie said as she came to stand over them. "What's going on here? What is all the—Shocker!"

She knelt down and lifted Shocker from Chance's arms. "Who did this?"

Chance looked up and saw, as he knew he would, Superion and his Invincibles standing among the crowd, smiles on their faces.

"Superion!" Throwing caution to the wind, Chance hurled himself at Superion. The Dark Thing caught him in midleap. He seemed to have appeared from nowhere.

"Let me go!" Chance screamed as he struggled in the Board Member's arms. "He did this! Let me go! I'm going to—!"

"You're going to what?" The Dark Thing growled. "Get yourself expelled? Fine then. Be my guest."

Calm down, Chance.

Chance heard Psy-chick's words at his mind's periphery as she, S.C., and P.J. came up to him. *He's right. Getting us barred from battle competition is exactly what Superion would want.*

Chance stopped struggling. But he stood there, his body tense, ready to pounce at any moment.

"These are serious accusations you're making, Mr. Fortune," Metatron said. The Invincibles's angelic combat instructor joined his team on the dance floor. "Do you have any proof?"

"Mind-scan them!" Psy-chick said. "That's all the proof—"

"You will not speak to me in such a disrespectful tone, Ms. Psy-chick!" Metatron said, ruffling his wings. "And not that I need to explain myself to you, but an in-depth psi-scan of a student outside of battle conditions must by authorized by the Academy Board!"

Metatron turned his attention back to Chance. "I ask you again, Mr. Fortune, do you have any proof of your accusations?"

Chance didn't answer. He stood, chest heaving with anger as he stared into Superion's smiling face.

"As I thought," Metatron said.

"Rest assured," Steel Valkyrie said to Metatron, "we shall

see what Mr. Shocker has to say about the matter when he comes to."

The supernurses arrived and took Shocker from Steel Valkyrie's arms. They laid him onto a clinic stretcher.

"Most certainly," Xenoman said as he materialized among them. "But for now, Steel Valkyrie, Metatron—I suggest you see your battle teams back to their dorm rooms for the night. If he's up to it, I will speak with Mr. Shocker in the morning, personally."

"Outlaws—let's go," Steel Valkyrie said. All The Outlaws but Chance turned and followed her. "Mr. Fortune, now!"

Chance stood a moment longer facing off with Superion. Then both team captains turned and followed their battle instructors out of the room.

That night, during the few hours Chance actually slept, the only dreams he had were of Shocker's broken body and Superion's smiling, triumphant face.

The next day, Shocker stood in Xenoman's office. He had one arm in a sling, a white strip of medical tape across his forehead covering three stitches, busted lips, and bruises around his eye sockets fading from blue to purple beneath his sunglasses. He'd chosen not to have an extended stay at Burlington's clinic as it would have put The Outlaws behind in TCT competition. Other than the arm, the wounds were more superficial than they appeared.

"You understand I could get the Board's authorization to

psi-scan you for the identity of the person responsible for this?" Xenoman asked.

"But you won't," Shocker said. "Will you, sir?"

"Against my better judgment," Xenoman said, "but there is something I'd like to show you." He began to get up from behind his desk when a loud knock sounded from the closed door of his office. He quickly slid back down into his seat, a perturbed look upon his face. "Come in."

Chance peeked his head in through the doorway.

"Sorry to interrupt, sir," Chance said. "But we've got TCT competition in five minutes. Is it okay if I steal Shocker away from you?"

Xenoman considered this for a moment. "I guess we're done here—for now." Before he'd finished, Shocker was out of his seat and at the door.

"Shocker," Xenoman said. "After TCT I'd still like to sho—"

"Sorry, Mr. Z," Shocker said as he skirted out the door. "But I got holotexts and studies and fights and stuff. With all that and my weakened condition, I think it's best I rest in the dorm room after class for the next few weeks, don't youokaythanksbye!"

The door closed, leaving Xenoman by himself. But not alone. Not anymore. Not ever again.

"So what's he going to do?" Chance asked as they walked out of Xenoman's office.

"Nothing," Shocker said.

"*Nothing?*" Chance asked. "Didn't you tell him?"

"Nope," Shocker said. "Not a word."

"Why not?" Chance asked in disbelief.

"I ain't no rat," Shocker said.

"But, Shocker—!"

"I said, I ain't no rat!"

They walked in silence for several seconds.

"Besides," Shocker said, "Superion almost killed Creeper and they didn't do a thing! You think the Academy is going to risk losing his father's contributions over me? A mortal? A nobody?"

Chance shrugged. "You're right, Shocker. If Superion's ever going to get what's coming to him, sooner or later, we're going to have to be the ones who give it to him!"

Chance and Shocker reached Kirby Coliseum to see a crowd of students gathered at the side of the cubed structure. They eased their way through the crowd to join the rest of The Outlaws. Chance looked at his teammates' faces. They were worried and confused.

"What's up?" Chance asked.

Psy-chick looked at him and then nodded in the coliseum's direction. Chance turned to see several supernurses in capes and masks phase through the coliseum wall. They carried several injured students on hoverstretchers.

Chance recognized one of them and rushed to his side.

"Nightwolf! What happened?" Chance exclaimed.

Nightwolf did not answer. He was unconscious and breathing through a respirator. Chance thought that was probably for the best as the wolfboy looked to be in bad shape.

"Is he going to be okay?" Chance asked one of the supernurses, his voice sharp with fear.

"We'll have him fixed up in no time." The supernurse gently pushed Chance away from the stretcher. "With the powers and technology available to us at the clinic, we can work wonders!"

At that moment, Alpha-Man came streaking out of the sky to land before the crowd. "Not to worry, students," he said. "Just a small accident. It seems the battle terrain MOTHER chose was a little more dangerous than expected."

"I thought MOTHER's safety protocols prevented this kind of stuff!" Shocker shouted.

"Yes, er, well," Alpha-Man said, "you bring up a good point. It appears MOTHER is experiencing technical difficulties. But Dr. Bryson assures me he'll have her back online and good as new by tomorrow. In the meantime, TCT is canceled for today. Why don't you all go home and catch up on your studies. Good day, everyone."

With that, Alpha-Man was gone again, rocketing off for the stratosphere.

"This is very weird," Space Cadet said. "MOTHER hasn't malfunctioned to this degree since coming online three decades ago. With the number of backup systems and security software she employs, the odds of something like this happening are, well, astronomical!"

The trash piles and now this! Chance thought. *What is wrong with this place?*

Xenoman rose from his chair and pressed a button on his desk. The lights dimmed and steel panels sprang from the walls to cover the office door and windows. His desk retracted into the floor and was replaced by a large computer terminal. The walls split open to reveal large monitors and other technologically advanced equipment. Xenoman now stood in what looked like the bridge of a starship.

Xenoman activated his powers of teleportation and then opened his cloak. The Hawaiian-shirted boy stood before him. The boy paid the professor no mind. He walked forward and pressed one of the buttons on the computer terminal. A hologram of what looked like a man in a black, hooded robe filled the room.

"Report!" the man in black spat.

The boy opened his mouth impossibly wide into a gaping maw. A nonsensical language of shrieks and moans issued from his throat.

"So," the robed man said, "you have yet to find the Key. The master will be terribly disappointed."

More horrible shrieking issued from the boy's mouth.

"No excuses!" the man snapped. "Our intell is flawless! The Key is at Burlington! I don't care how many unnecessary assimilations you must conduct, the Key must be found!"

The boy uttered several more sanity-rending moans.

"Yes, well," the man in black said, "such hiccups in campus routine are to be expected. Your methods are hardly—precise."

The boy shrieked in response.

"I told the master he should have sent me. What's needed there is a scalpel, not a broadsword. Regardless, just so long as no one suspects. . . . And if anyone begins to entertain any thoughts in that regard—you know what to do!"

17

Over the next two months, the feud between The Outlaws and The Invincibles escalated. After the attack on Shocker, The Invincibles knew better than to push their luck with any further outright physical assault. But the sneers and trash talking between the teams became so ferocious that it engulfed the entire school. Battle lines were drawn within the student body. The Invincibles's supporters, consisting mostly of demigods, on one side—versus The Outlaws's supporters, typically mortals and adventurers, on the other.

When December arrived, it was no surprise to anyone at Burlington Academy that The Invincibles and The Outlaws were the two teams going head-to-head in the TCT finals. With the loss of Creeper putting The Lost Boys out of competition, The Invincibles and The Outlaws had the two best battle records on campus.

On the night before the battle, Chance sat alone in one of

Grant VR Library's study rooms going over battle scenarios. He was so engrossed in his studies, he failed to hear Superion enter and sit down across from him.

"Well, well," Superion said, his tone mocking. "Here I am face-to-face with Chance Fortune, leader of The Outlaws, the luckiest person alive! Well, Fortune, your luck just ran out."

"Get out!" Chance leapt from his seat, ready to fight.

"Please," Superion said, raising his hand. "I could squash you like a grape faster than a brain synapse, and we both know it. Besides, I'm not here to fight you, Fortune. No, I'm here to do you a favor."

Chance stared unblinking at the Invincible.

"I'm here to reason with you," Superion said. "Why don't you save us all some trouble and forfeit. You can't really hope to beat us. I mean, look at you. You and your team are a veritable freak show. Face it, Fortune, your Outlaws consist of a spineless teacher's pet, a blubbersome geek, a juvenile delinquent, a goth weirdo, daddy's little princess—"

Superion crossed his arms.

"And you. Your powers amount to nothing at all. You are but a bug to be ground beneath my heel. Only Iron Maiden is worthy of my notice, although she has relinquished that privilege simply in befriending you. Forfeit and save yourself unnecessary embarrassment. You know I speak the truth."

Chance looked Superion up and down, noting the corded muscles capable of crushing boulders into powder, the steel blue eyes able to see amoebas divide, and his resolve wavered. Here and now, Superion did seem invincible.

Maybe he's right, Chance thought. *Maybe I have gotten by so far on sheer dumb luck. I don't have any superpowers, after all. I never have. Maybe tomorrow I'll be found out for the fraud that I am. How could I have ever dreamed I could be a superhero, much less lead a team of them?*

No reason for my friends to suffer for my inadequacies. Better not even to bother. Better not to subject them or myself to the pain and humiliation of defeat.

Superion rose from his seat. "I'll take your silence to mean you are, at the least, considering what I've said. By all means, I encourage you to think it over."

He walked toward the door and it slid open for him. He paused and turned to look back at Chance.

"With enough thought, you'll see that giving up is the only logical path open to you. Ta-ta, Fortune."

With mere hours to go before the contest, Chance was nowhere to be found. This information was leaked to the outside world, and odds already calculated at a million to one on gambling holoboards hidden throughout Megalopolis escalated even further in Superion's favor.

As time for the championship bout between The Outlaws and The Invincibles drew nearer, both The Outlaws and The Lost Boys began searching for Chance. Whether by luck, fate, divine intervention, or a mixture of all of the above, it was Psy-chick who happened upon him. She found Chance skipping pebbles across the phosphorous pool of Simpson Gardens.

"We've been looking everywhere for you," Psy-chick said, taking a seat beside Chance at the pool's edge.

"I know how to stay hidden when I don't want to be found," Chance replied, not taking his eyes from the pond.

"Oh, so now you do want to be found?" Psy-chick asked, nudging Chance in the ribs with her elbow, trying to get a smile out of him. He ignored the gesture and skipped another pebble across the pond. It bounced several times and then dropped into the decorative wooden bucket at the foot of a stone well on the pond's other side.

"Chance, it doesn't take an empath to understand how you must be feeling—"

"You have no idea how I'm feeling!" Chance snapped.

Psy-chick sighed. "That's true. Those mental defenses of yours are as strong as ever. So then tell me. How are you feeling?"

Chance skipped more pebbles across the pond. Each finished its trek by dropping into the bucket he'd placed on the opposite shore.

Psy-chick sat in silence, waiting until Chance was ready to speak. After some time, he did.

"I can't beat him," Chance said. Psy-chick kept silent, giving Chance the opportunity to say everything he was thinking. "I've come all this way, only to fail. I'm an idiot. Just like he was."

"Just like who, Chance?"

A large boulder of emotion inside Chance began to move. He sat still and quiet, trying to halt its progress. But the pain was too much.

"Have I ever told you about my father, Psy-chick?"

She shook her head.

"No? Well, there's a reason. John was his name, but everybody called him Project. When I was a kid, everywhere we'd go, all you'd hear was, 'How you doing, Project? Oh, that's a mighty fine-looking boy you've got there, Project.'

"I didn't think anything about it back then. I was a kid after all, and that's all I'd ever heard him called. It just seemed natural to me. I mean, I called him Project as much as I called him Dad, myself."

Psy-chick nodded, gesturing for Chance to continue.

"It wasn't until a few years later I learned how he got his nickname. Dad grew up in Littleton. Apparently, even as a boy he was always a daydreamer—saying he was going to climb Mount Everest one month, swim the Atlantic Ocean the next. That's an exaggeration, but you get the picture. He was always gung-ho about some *project* he was doing or planning on doing.

"Of course, each one would fail. Again and again and again. But it was like he had selective memory. Last month's endeavor would be over, forgotten, the time and energy he'd wasted on it forgotten, too."

Tears began to leak from Chance's eyes. He removed his mask so it wouldn't get wet, then spoke.

"Unfortunately for Mom and me, he was the same way as an adult. I remember him coming home to announce that he'd quit his job time after time, but the one he had lined up was going to take him to the top! This was going to be *the one*!

"But *the one* never seemed to come. I spent the first six years of my life living in little more than a shack. It was horrible. I remember waking up one night when I was four and feeling something nibbling at my toes. I threw back the covers. There were mice everywhere. Not just one or two, but a lot!

"I screamed and screamed. Momma ran into my room, followed by Dad, and flipped on the light. She screamed, too, but snatched me out of bed and ran into the living room. It was the only time I ever saw her chew my father out for being the loser that he was."

Chance skipped another pebble into the bucket. Psy-chick waited, listening.

"Ironically enough, things seemed to turn around after that. A prominent car manufacturer decided to build a plant in Littleton and Dad gave up his ways for a steady job and a decent income. It appeared he actually had found *the one.*

"We bought the house we live in now. Mom got pregnant with Jacob. We were well on our way to becoming one big happy family. Of course, ol' Project couldn't have that, now, could he?"

The emotional rock inside Chance slid a notch, drawing closer to an edge within him.

"The company invested heavily in a new computer system on his recommendation. Dad had no doubt it was going to revolutionize the business. Project was made project head, just as he'd always wanted to be. The only problem was that after the system was instituted, it never really worked. Dad was fired, his reputation ruined. Finding other work was impossible.

"Eventually, he quit trying. He just sat around the house. He hardly bathed. Hardly ate. Hardly did anything. Jacob was around now, and if money had been tight before, it was in a choke hold now."

The boulder of emotion inside Chance teetered on edge, ready to fall at any moment.

"I was eight when they pulled our car out of the river. Dad had taken out quite a substantial life insurance policy when he'd been with the company. Amazingly, the premiums had been kept up to date—and suicide could never be proven. Even though his body was never found, the insurance company had to pay out."

The anger, the hate, and the regret balled up inside Chance fell, smashing itself into a thousand shards of pain and loss. He scowled and slung the pebble in his hand so hard it shot across the pond and struck the bucket, knocking it over, spilling its contents.

"So you see, Psy-chick," Chance said, "I'm doomed to failure! Predestined to crash and burn! It's in my genes, my blood. There's no point in me facing Superion. He'd just eat me alive. *I don't have a chance.* I was stupid to ever think I could make it here. I was stupid to think I could be a superhero! I'm just ol' Project all over again!"

Chance turned to face Psy-chick. Tears flowed down his face and when he spoke, his voice wavered.

"I'm dropping out of school, so you don't have to be around me. Don't worry, I wouldn't dream of dragging you and the team down in the muck like he did Momma and me. This is one miserable failure who doesn't want the people he cares about to suffer because of him!"

Psy-chick slipped an arm around Chance. She let her feelings for him seep out through her fingertips and into him. Little by little, she opened her heart, washing him in a steady, ever-increasing flow of positive emotion.

"Chance, how can you say you're a failure? You've been nothing but a success since you came here. Look at all you've accomplished! You've made a winning team out of a crew who otherwise wouldn't give a flarn about this school, one another, or even themselves. Even better, you've made us a family. Each and every one of us would do anything for you, Chance. To quit on us now would be a slap in our faces!"

Chance frowned.

"And not just to us either, Chance," Psy-chick said. "I hear the thoughts of mortals and adventurers all across campus you don't even know about. They idolize you! You are one of them—one of *us*—who's made it! You give us hope. You help us dream. You show us what we can be if we only believe in ourselves and give it our all! If that doesn't make you a superhero, then I don't know what does!

"I know how hard this battle could be—especially for you, our captain—and I want nothing more than to tell you to forget about it and run away and stay safe forever!"

He turned and looked her in the eye. There Chance saw adoration, compassion, and belief. Belief in him. But beyond all those, Chance saw wisdom—wisdom equal to anything he'd ever seen in his mother's eyes, or even the Captain's.

"You are not your father," Psy-chick said. *"You are Chance Fortune!* And running away is not something Chance Fortune does. The words *give up* are not in his vocabulary. And it

doesn't matter if he falls flat on his face again and again. He gets back up each and every time."

For the first time since Psy-chick sat down beside him, Chance smiled. He was grateful for Psy-chick's friendship and realized it was a greater thing than any superpower ever imagined. Without exactly realizing what he was doing, Chance found himself leaning his head toward Psy-chick's. His heart began to pound as he saw her also leaning toward him, her eyes closing, her lips—!

"To think we've been worried about you," Shocker said, walking up behind them, the rest of The Outlaws following in his wake.

Chance and Psy-chick awoke as if from a trance and scrambled to their feet, their cheeks reddening.

"And all this time," Shocker continued, "you've just been up here honeybunning—"

Shocker's hands clamped over his mouth before he could finish his sentence.

"Be nice, Shocker," Psy-chick said. Shocker's hands exploded from his face as Psy-chick released her telekinetic hold on them.

Chance looked to Psy-chick, smiled, and addressed the team.

"I'm sorry I wimped out on you guys for a while," he said, his face becoming serious. "It won't happen again. I promise."

"No need to apologize, Chance," Gothika said.

"We knew you wouldn't let us down," S.C. said.

"Guys," Chance said, "I'm going to need your help. I have some ideas about a few *extras* that might give us a slight advantage over Superion."

"Isn't that cheating?" Iron Maiden asked.

"Not cheating," P.J. said, smiling, "assessing the situation and then doing what needs to be done. Right, Chance?"

Chance grinned as he nodded to Private Justice.

"Lead the way, Hicksville," Shocker said. "Lead the way."

"Okay," S.C. said as he motioned to the equipment strewn across a hovertable in his dorm room. "What you've got here is your standard package of explosives, stunners, sonics, and smart weapons."

"Flarn, pud," Shocker said, reaching for one of the displayed items. "You could overthrow a small country with this stuff!"

"Ah-ah-ah!" S.C. warned. "Don't touch that! It'd blow half of the campus to smithereens!" Shocker gulped, his eyes wide, and eased his hand from the table.

"Too bad it's Superion we've got to go up against," P.J. said.

Iron Maiden smacked P.J. on the back of his head like a big sister disciplining her tactless younger brother.

"Hey, hey, hey," Gothika chided. "We'll have no naysayers on this boat!"

"Sorry," P.J. said.

"P.J.'s right," Chance said. "Superion will be tough. But hopefully this stuff will give us the edge when we need it."

"But this, Chance," S.C. said, "is the coup de grâce!" He extracted a wrist gauntlet from the table and handed it to Chance. "Here, put this on."

Chance placed the gauntlet around his forearm. It was

adorned with a keypad familiar to him, though he couldn't quite place where he'd seen it before.

"It's a D.S. Agent stealth gauntlet," S.C. said, answering Chance's unspoken query. "Shocker was able to get it from Moore Museum."

"How'd you get the museum to loan you a piece of DSA armor?" Iron Maiden asked.

"Well," Shocker said, "I didn't exactly ask for permission."

Iron Maiden gasped. But then she returned his smile in kind. "You mean you stole it?"

"I prefer to think of it as a long-term loan," Shocker said with a wink.

"Remember us geeking out over your studies of Socs physiology?" S.C. asked Chance.

"Soshawho?" Gothika asked.

"Superion's people, his race, the Socs."

"Leave it to you two to crack the holotexts even after your homework's done," Shocker said, rolling his eyes. "I can't tell you guys how many dissertations I've had to endure from Chance about Andromedan philosophy!"

"I remembered you once told me," S.C. said, never minding the interruption, "that despite their various super-visions, Socs can't see electromagnetic energy above X-rays or below microwaves in the light spectrum. I've modified this stealth control to encompass light waves even beyond those ranges."

"In English, S.C.," Gothika said.

"For all intents and purposes, when Chance activates this gauntlet, Superion won't be able to see him no matter what kind of super-vision he throws at him!"

Space Cadet tapped several keys on the gauntlet's control pad and blue sparks surged the length of Chance's body. The air shimmered around Chance and then he was gone. A second later he reappeared on the room's other side.

"S.C.," Chance said, "I know you won't let me, but if I could, I really would kiss you!"

"Well, *I'm* going to," Psy-chick said and then planted a big smooch on S.C.'s cheek.

S.C. stared wide-eyed at nothing for a long time, a huge smile across his chubby ebony face.

18

Chance left the dorm room ahead of his friends. He wanted to get to their locker room in the coliseum early for some last-minute meditation, his calm time before the storm. Chance grimaced and held his nose as he exited the dorm to see heaping piles of trash littering the green. He waded through the garbage, making his way across campus. The main thoroughfare was so thick with debris that he decided to take a shortcut. He turned down the alleyway between McFarlane Cafeteria and the Grant VR Library. Chance halted in his steps when he looked down the alley to see the enormous back of Xenoman.

The Board Member held out his arms, spreading his cloak's full width out to either side of him. Chance couldn't see what was on the other side of the professor's cape, but he heard what sounded like a thousand slimy worms wriggling over one another.

"Hey!" Chance called out.

Xenoman slammed his cloak shut and whirled to face Chance. The slithering noise simultaneously ceased.

Chance now saw numerous students standing behind the professor, the Hawaiian-shirted boy among them. He remembered that the boy had been the first student he'd met after teleporting to campus. He recalled how the boy had seized him, looked him over, and then dismissed him. *And now I find him here in this strange situation.*

"What were you doing, sir?" Chance asked Xenoman.

"None of your concern, Mr. Fortune," Xenoman snapped. "I believe you have a championship to attend?"

Xenoman stepped aside to allow Chance passage. The students behind him did likewise, moving like a formation of soldiers to create a path between them.

Not knowing what else to do, Chance crept down the walkway between them. The students stood in silence, so still even their breathing was imperceptible.

Now, this is just weird, Chance thought.

Chance walked ten yards beyond the group and then turned to face them. They all stood watching him, not a word being spoken among them. The Hawaiian-shirted boy stood between them and Chance like a mother bear protecting her cubs.

It's as though he were their—leader. And he's daring me to interfere. But interfere with what?

Chance took a few steps backward and then turned around, resuming his trek toward the coliseum.

I think I'll mention this to Steel Valkyrie, Chance thought. *As soon as the championship's over, of course.*

But Chance never had the opportunity to talk in-depth with his combat instructor. Perhaps if he had, he would have been spared the horror that was to come.

Chance reached Kirby Coliseum and went around back to take a secret entrance only he knew about. Or so he thought. Block was leaning against the building, twirling a small gray capsule on the end of a chain around his finger. His other hand was held behind his back.

"Thought I'd find you here," The Lost Boys's captain said.

"Block," Chance said, shaking his friend's rocky hand. "I'm certainly surprised to see you!"

"Come on, Fortune," Block said. "You didn't think I'd let my roomie go off to war without wishing him luck, did you? Not that you're going to need it. Not now, anyway."

"What's that?" Chance asked, pointing to the twirling capsule.

"Why, it's your ace in the hole, Fortune," Block said, bringing the capsule to rest in his hand. "It's what brings me here. I've put my heart and soul into it, you might say."

"Pardon?" Chance asked.

"It's a little piece of me," Block said, smiling. He brought his other hand out from behind his back. A bandage was wrapped around one of the large rocky digits. Chance saw it was partially soaked with Block's fluorescent green blood.

"A little piece of my achillesheelenite hide, anyway," he continued, "encased in this lead capsule." Block unscrewed the small cylinder's lid and let Chance have a look at the pebble of his skin inside before screwing the lid back on.

"I want you to use it against Superion. This should be enough to keep him from getting too close." Block's eyes hardened. "But if I were you, I'd let him get close. He'll want to grab you by the neck and gloat. That's when I'd shove it down his throat! That'd put him down for the count!"

"I don't know, Block," Chance said. "I'm already stretching the rules as it is. But this is the direct use of someone else's superpower. I appreciate the gesture, man. Really, I do! But I just don't think I should."

Block looked Chance in the eye, his expression as serious as a gravestone. He held the capsule out to Chance.

"For Creeper—and Shocker. Pay Superion back!"

Chance stared at the small cylinder long and hard. He took it from Block's hand.

Block nodded. "Good luck, Chance." Then he headed back toward the dorm to catch the championship on holodisplay.

Chance watched his friend depart, mulling over what he'd just agreed to. *Hopefully it won't come to that,* Chance thought. He put the chain around his neck and stuffed the capsule riding upon it down the throat of his bodysuit.

Chance phased through Kirby Coliseum's outer wall and entered The Outlaws's locker room. He found an area partitioned off from the remaining room and settled into his relaxation exercises. He was still there an hour later trying to calm himself when he heard his teammates come in and sit down to talk among themselves. Like him, they were feeling anxious and uncertain.

"Where's Chance?" S.C. asked.

"Thought he was coming with you, pud," Shocker said.

"You don't think he—?" Iron Maiden began.

"Chance? Our captain?" Private Justice interrupted. "No way! Not after this morning."

"You couldn't blame him," Gothika said. "I keeping thinking about what happened to Creeper, myself."

Get out there, Chance thought. *Calm them down. Psych them up. Be a leader!*

But his eyes refused to open and his legs refused to move. If he did either, it meant this was all real. If Chance got up, he could no longer pretend that he was back in Littleton where his biggest worry was what movie he was going to watch on holovision that afternoon. If Chance got up, he had to face his teammates and his responsibility to them. If Chance got up, he had to face Superion.

"Chance promised he wouldn't let us down," Psy-chick said. "He will be here."

Chance smiled. *Thank goodness for Psy-chick.* And as though her voice were the kiss in some fairy tale where the beauty awakens the sleeping prince, Chance opened his eyes and rose to his feet.

"I'm here," Chance called as he came out from behind the partition. He radiated confidence and determination as he greeted each of his teammates.

"P.J.?"

Private Justice jumped to his feet and snapped off a salute. "Locked, cocked, and ready to rock, sir! Uh, I mean, Chance."

"You flowing, Gothika?"

"I'm feeling better now that we're all here. And trust me, Gaea herself doesn't know the magic I'm about to unleash!"

"Got your gear, S.C.?"

"Dilithium crystals at full capacity, Captain! I've been waiting all morning to say that!"

"You juiced, Shocker?"

"Like an orange grove, Hicksville!"

"A lot's resting on you today, Iron Maiden," Chance said. "I know you're up to it, though. Yeah—that's the spirit! Just imagine that steel bar you just bent is Superion's head."

How you are you, Psy-chick? Chance thought to Psy-chick.

Great, now that my captain is here to lead, Psy-chick thought to Chance.

They smiled at each other. Then Chance turned to face his team.

"Well—I haven't a thing to say. You all know the drill, what needs to be done. Each and every one of you've worked your butts off to get us here. Whatever happens today, you're already champions. However—

"Many on campus think we can't beat The Invincibles. They've already decided our run, while a good one, is at an end. Well, I say to heck with what they think! We've made them eat crow pie all semester! Today won't be any different. Like a good friend of mine once said, no matter how powerful The Invincibles may seem, we've got a weapon more awesome than they could ever dream of! We've got one another. *And that makes us invincible!* You're the best battle team a captain could ever ask for—" Chance paused. "—and—and the best friends, too."

Chance gasped, shocked when Space Cadet ran face-first into his stomach and flung his arms around his waist in a large bear hug. Then Psy-chick's arms were around their shoulders. Then Iron Maiden's. Then Gothika's. Shocker even joined in. Then Private Justice's elongated arms wound around them all.

Chance led his team out onto the Infinity Chamber's ramp. The Invincibles were already positioned around their side of the Infinity Posts, sneering and taunting, laughing and pointing.

"Fat Chance Fortune!" the trench-coated Mindbender taunted.

"I'm going to run circles around you Outlosers!" Speed De-mon cackled. His laughter caused the tiny horns of his devil costume to shake.

"Would you like another dance, Shocker?" Delilah snapped her whip.

"I'm going to have such fun making each of you powerless!" the vampirelike Raz said.

Warlock looked directly at Chance, pointed to his own yel-low eyes, and then stuck his fingers out at Chance. *I'm watch-ing you.*

Ratticus swished his tail and wrung his paws as he hissed with laughter.

Superion stepped forward, his usual smug smile plastered across his face. Chance could almost feel the godling's microscopic vision scanning him, dissecting his person at the molecular level. Chance met him near the Infinity Posts.

"Well, well," Superion said, his tone mocking. "Decided to show up after all, eh? I should've known you'd be that stupid, Fortune."

Chance felt Psy-chick's hand slip into his. She squeezed it hard. Chance squeezed back as he looked into her beautiful, resolute eyes—eyes that made him swell with renewed confidence.

Then another hand took his left, and Iron Maiden stood beside him. One by one the rest of The Outlaws clasped hands, even Shocker, until they stood as a family, defiant in the face of Superion and his Invincibles.

"I hope the seat of your tights is well padded, Superion," Chance said. "Because we are about to kick—your—butt!"

Superion huffed, then wheeled around to rejoin his team. Chance led The Outlaws back to their place along the platform's edge as the Infinity Posts began to power up, their violet energy running up their lengths to resonate within the twin bulbed heads cresting them.

"The Team Combat-Combat-Combat," MOTHER said, her voice skipping like a scratched CD. "One-zero-one-one. Systems error. Reboot."

There was a pause and then MOTHER continued.

"As I was saying, the Team Combat Training Championship will consist of a Snatch-and-Grab scenario encompassing two objectives. The first objective is the infiltration of this fortress housed inside the depths of an active volcano."

A large hologram featuring the cross-section of a mountain volcano shimmered into being. A large citadel was encased inside its core.

"The second objective—the fortress's power circuit," MOTHER said, "is located within the mountain's core. The first team to remove the circuit and deactivate the fortress and its subunits will be the winner. Good luck to you all."

With MOTHER's last words, the Infinity Posts sparked and then lightning crackled between them.

"Where angels fear to tread, Hicksville!" Shocker screamed to Chance over the energy's roar.

"Where angels fear to tread!" Chance answered.

Then reality twisted around them.

19

The glaring light faded to reveal laser fire from flying fighter ships and hordes of robots on sky skimmers raining down upon both teams. The skimmers were little more than flying snowboards, but the ships loomed above like dark, gigantic thunderheads.

"Take cover!" Chance shouted. And they did, ducking down behind the overturned cars and crumbling skyscrapers of the abandoned postapocalyptic city to which MOTHER had transported them. But not before each was able to see the smoking volcano towering above the city off in the distance.

Psy-chick. Chance pushed the words outside his mental barrier so Psy-chick could receive them. *Go ahead and open the telepathic link between the team so we can all communicate freely.*

Done, Psy-chick thought back to him.

That's where we've got to get to, gang. Chance broadcasted a mental image of the volcano. *I'm sure The Invincibles are* heading straight for it, trying to hack their way through the ships and robots. We'll let them draw the bulk of the fire while we sneak around to the volcano's rear. We'll punch through inside there.

S.C., do you think you could modify the stealth gauntlet so that it projects a field that would cloak us all?

Space Cadet thought, *I'll give it my best—*

What's that, S.C.? I didn't copy the last. But S.C.'s thoughts didn't come. No one's did. Then Chance heard a scream—a girl's scream—Psy-chick's scream!

Chance leapt out from behind his boulder to see Raz holding Psy-chick by her wrists. Ratticus was at his side, a malicious grin adorning his rodent face. Chance watched as Ratticus smacked Psy-chick across the top of her head with his fleshy tail, rendering her unconscious. Raz let her drop to the ground to lie at his feet.

"That will be enough of that, little princess," Raz hissed.

Chance cursed as he ran toward them. He ducked and rolled in midsprint just in time to dodge a barrage of Shocker's blue-white energy bolts. He hit the ground and looked up to see Delilah's leather whip wound around his teammate's neck.

I'm so stupid, Chance thought. *I should have known! I should have factored in The Invincibles's arrogance! So confident are they that they'll reach the power circuit before us, they're not even trying for it, but just hanging around to pick us off instead! The strategy I planned is useless!*

Iron Maiden crashed through the skyscraper's side, enormous clouds of dust, debris, and shrapnel following in her wake. She plunged in and out of another building and then another before she hit the street, churning up a trail of pavement a quarter mile long before her momentum gave out and she came to a halt.

A red-and-blue comet zoomed down toward her, threatening to smash her into oblivion. The comet stopped just short of Iron Maiden, revealing itself to be Superion.

"Must we go on with this pointless bout of fisticuffs, Maiden?" Superion asked.

Iron Maiden's answer was a right cross to Superion's jaw. He hurtled head over heels high into the air, crashing through several fighter ships, and then down on an automobile. The vehicle's windows exploded outward in a million pieces as he impacted.

"Very well," Superion said as he got to his feet. "It's your funeral!"

Gothika stood unmoving, her wrists crossed before the glowing ankh at her chest, as laser beams from the fighter ships and skimmers flying above defied the laws of physics and bent harmlessly around her to churn up the pavement at her feet. She watched as Warlock approached her, his face serene, the same lasers passing through his celestial body as though it were vapor.

"Merry meet, Gothika," Warlock said as he came to a halt several yards before her.

"Merry meet, Warlock," Gothika said.

"Because you are my sister in the universal coven," Warlock said, "I extend to you this opportunity to yield. I am already a fifth-level adept. I can sense you are merely a third. Surrender. You cannot beat me."

"Flarn you!" Gothika said as plumes of flame shot from her hand to engulf Warlock. A few seconds later the pyre dissipated to reveal an unharmed but annoyed Warlock.

"Balefire?" Warlock asked. "How childish. As you wish, then."

The yellow light in Warlock's eyes magnified in intensity until they became shining twin stars. The air around the two combatants shimmered as if distorted by heat while bolts of mystical energy discharged from Warlock's body. Small pebbles and bits of rubble rose into the wavering air, carried upward by some unseen but palpable force. Warlock grinned as uncertainty crept over Gothika's face.

"Now," Warlock said, "you shall witness the devastating power of a sorcerer born of the line of Maerlyn!"

The car dropped from the sky, its shadow expanding over Private Justice's horror-stricken face as he stood in the middle of the city street. The vehicle landed, flattening P.J.—literally—before smashing down onto him again and again, accompanied by the sound of shrill laughter.

"I could do this all day," Mindbender said, guffawing. He held his hands over his trench-coated gut as if it pained him to laugh. "And I think I will! Is this how you got that flattop anyway? You're like a life-size rubber chicken, Justice! A big dumb joke!"

The black-and-crimson blur that was Speed Demon raced out of the city, zipping effortlessly around enemy fire from the multiple skycraft. He sped up the volcano's side and paused at its rim to survey the situation. Through the black smoke rising into the twilight sky, Speed Demon saw a blanket of shimmering molten rock covering the volcano's mouth.

No good there, Speed Demon thought, and then was moving once more, running down the volcano's side at mach speed. He darted here and there, to and fro, searching every nook, cranny, cave, and crevice. At every turn he found magma and its unbearable heat barred his way. Speed Demon cursed. Left with no alternative, he headed back toward the city to find his captain.

Iron Maiden lifted a garbage truck over her head and flung it at Superion. It smashed into him, knocking him into an abandoned building. The building collapsed, burying Superion under a pile of rubble and sending enormous clouds of dust billowing skyward.

Nothing moved. The dusted settled. Iron Maiden sighed in relief. The battle was over and she had won. She was turning to rejoin her team when the ground beneath her shook. A moment later, the pile of rubble exploded, knocking her to the ground.

The dust cleared to reveal Superion. He flew toward Iron Maiden at unquantifiable speed, enveloping her in a whirlwind of punches, kicks, heat vision, and blizzard-cold breath.

"What has become of you, Iron Maiden?" Superion asked. "I know your mother forced you to stay on their team, but how could you actually yield leadership to a mere mortal? No, not even a mortal—*an adventurer*? It's as though you've accepted Fortune and the rest as equals!"

Iron Maiden tried to voice a reply, but what came out was a moan of pain as Superion held her bruised, bloodied, and semiconscious body by the throat.

Speed Demon zoomed up to his team captain.

"What are you doing here?" Superion asked. "Your assignment was to disengage the volcano fortress's power circuit!"

"That's what I came to tell you, Superion," Speed Demon said. "I can't get in. There's a protective magma flow surrounding the fortress. I tried every entrance on that mountain but they're all covered by it!"

Superion sighed in exasperation. "Must I do everything? I will handle the circuit. You see to the fat one. He's unoccupied at the moment."

Speed Demon was off, a light contrail following in his wake.

"Delilah!" Superion called. Delilah, her whip still wound around Shocker's neck, turned her attention to her captain. "Dispose of this mortal-lover!" He flung Iron Maiden the distance between them. She landed in a crumpled heap at Delilah's feet. "I have a championship to win."

Superion rocketed skyward toward the volcano.

Warlock uncrossed his arms, throwing them down and out at his sides. The unseen force discharged in the process galloped toward Gothika, its progress made visible by the clouds of dust and debris it kicked up along the street. It struck the Outlaw witch, the impact knocking her backward.

Cars and boulder-size chunks of rubble now rose into the shimmering air, their levitation charged by the extraneous amounts of magical force summoned by the dueling conjurers.

Gothika scooped up a handful of rocks and slung it at Warlock. Sailing through the air, the rocks transformed into basketball-size pterodactyls. They swarmed Warlock, biting and slashing him. He fell to the ground, rolling and thrashing in an attempt to fling them off.

"Enough!" Warlock yelled. His entire body exploded like a dwarf supernova, emitting a flash of light that seared the pterodactyl demons from existence. The shockwave sent Gothika and everything else nearby hurtling backward.

She lay on her back, bruised and bloodied, fighting not to lose consciousness. Warlock's shadow fell over her. She looked up at him. The wizard adept's entire body was smoking and he panted for breath as though he'd just run a hundred-mile marathon.

"I," Warlock said, "have—beaten you—witch. Surrender

your amulet. It is my right!" He held out his hand, eyeing the ankh at Gothika's throat.

Gothika groaned as she struggled to her knees. She stared up at Warlock, scowling from her position of submission as she grasped the ankh and tore it from the band around her neck. Warlock grinned, eyeing his prize with greed. He motioned for Gothika to quit stalling and hand him the amulet. She gulped and held it out to him, her expression humbled. As Warlock reached down to take his trophy, it disappeared from Gothika's hand.

"What sorcery is this?" Warlock asked, his face full of angry disbelief.

"It's called sleight of hand, you poser! Here's another trick for you!" Gothika then closed her hand into a fist and punched Warlock in the stomach. The wizard adept sank to his knees, leaning over so his grimacing face was level to Gothika's. She reached behind his ear with her empty left hand and brought it back out for Warlock to view. It now held her ankh.

Gothika raised her eyebrows and smiled at him. "Those are the breaks!"

Warlock fell over, unconscious.

Iron Maiden lay in a crumpled mass at Delilah's feet. Delilah grinned like a child given a shiny new play toy. Forced to his knees by Delilah's whip, Shocker looked down at Iron Maiden. He'd been in desperate anticipation of Delilah's next command. He existed now only to please her. But looking at

Iron Maiden's bleeding, prostrate body, this compulsion wavered. Shocker liked Iron Maiden. Through a cloudy haze, he wondered why Superion would want Delilah to hurt her.

"Yes," Delilah hissed. "She's pretty, isn't she?"

Shocker nodded.

"You like her, don't you?"

Shocker nodded once more.

Delilah bent down so her face was next to Shocker's. "That is why," she cooed, "I'm going to have you blast her within inches of her life."

Iron Maiden lay there indifferent, too weak to move or protest. Shocker shook his head. "No. . ."

"What?" Delilah asked, her eyes wide in disbelief. She yanked the whip taut around his neck. "How dare you defy me! You will shock her! And you will do it now!"

Shocker whirled around to face Iron Maiden, raising his hands, moving like a puppet having its strings pulled. Beads of sweet budded across his forehead, soaking his bandanna.

"Do it!" Delilah commanded.

Shocker grimaced, his hands shaking, battling with himself. His hands powered up, emitting the blue glare that heralded the inevitable discharge of lightning. Iron Maiden closed her eyes, ready to receive the blast.

"Yes," Delilah said. "Do—"

Her words were cut short as Shocker reached up and grasped the whip wound around his neck. Hundreds of volts of electricity surged through it and into Delilah. She flew backward through the air, smoke and sparks of electricity trailing in her wake. She hit the ground unconscious several yards off in the distance.

Shocker bent down and helped Iron Maiden into a sitting position.

"That," Iron Maiden said, "was—incredible. Thank you."

Shocker searched for some arrogant yet witty reply, but in the end just said, "Don't mention it."

20

"Hey, Raz" Chance said.

Raz turned, a questioning expression on his face. Chance's right fist connected between Raz's eyes, sending him into darkness. As the negator's unconscious body dropped, Chance backflipped, dodging Ratticus's tail.

The rat-human hybrid retreated, taking a defensive stance, baring his claws and two front incisors in a show of menace. Not that it would do Ratticus any good, for he'd hurt Psychick, and nothing but his complete decimation would quell Chance's fury.

Chance charged toward Ratticus, an unstoppable force. The wererat scraped up rocks and chunks of debris with his claws and slung them at the Outlaw captain again and again. Without taking his icy gaze from Ratticus or slowing down, Chance drew his twin billy clubs and smashed the multiple projectiles into tiny pieces with preternatural speed and accuracy.

Trapped, Ratticus lunged in attack, his front teeth and claws headed straight for Chance's eyes. If Chance had been his usual calm self, he would have thought what a brainless and crude maneuver his opponent was executing. But Joyce Blevins's son was gone. Only the instinct-powered fighting machine remained.

Chance dealt a devastating blow to the side of Ratticus's muzzle with his club. Without hesitation, he spun 180 degrees, delivering a backhand blow to the side of Ratticus's skull. He leapt into the air and spun once more, this time executing a roundhouse kick. The attack sent Ratticus's unconscious body flying backward through the air.

Chance stood breathing heavily, more winded from his cold rage, now dissipating, than from the actual fight. He released his billy clubs, dropped to his knees beside Psy-chick, and pulled her head and shoulders into his lap.

Chance shook her. "Psy-chick—?"

She murmured incoherently, and then her eyes fluttered open. She looked up at Chance and smiled. The Invincibles, The Outlaws, the TCT Championship, the Academy, the entire world faded away. In that moment it was like he was seeing her for the first time all over again.

"Hey," Psy-chick said, sitting up. "Are you okay?"

"Uh, yeah," Chance said. "And here I thought I was rescuing you! But yeah, everything's fine—everything's wonderful!"

"*Oooookaaaaay*," Psy-chick said. She glanced over Chance's shoulder and saw two robots piloting skimmers sail downward through the air. With no time to warn Chance, telepathically or otherwise, she grabbed his shoulders and rolled behind a sheltering pile of rubble, pulling him down atop her as the skimmers' laser fire blasted the area where they had been lying only seconds before.

The robots soared upward to regroup for another shot. "Chance," Psy-chick said, "Don't you think we should get out of here before they come back? The team needs our help."

"Wha—?" Chance asked, swimming upward back to reality. "Oh, yeah. My bad." He shook himself as he got up and helped Psy-chick to her feet.

"What about them?" Psy-chick asked, gesturing to the unconscious Invincibles, Raz and Ratticus.

"Leave them," Chance said. "They'll be fine."

Chance and Psy-chick started for the battle. Then he stopped and looked back at the negator. "No! Wait! I've got a better idea!"

Mindbender cackled as he brought the now demolished car down on top of Private Justice for the hundredth time. "You know, Justice, there's nothing I like more than to cause others pain. And let me tell you, I haven't had this much fun in ages!"

As Mindbender lifted the car up yet again by the sheer power of his mind, a thought occurred to him. No, not just *a* thought, but *the* thought! The revelation! The epiphany he'd been searching for his entire life.

"Oh my!" Mindbender said. "Yes! Of course! Why didn't I think of it sooner?" He flung the car aside. It struck the pavement, and came to rest upside down in the street. Private Justice's body swelled, resuming its natural shape, now that it no longer had to contend with the car's onslaught. Mindbender took no notice, however.

"It's so obvious," Mindbender said. "The reason I'm here! The purpose for which I've been born! I am ready to fulfill my destiny!

He picked up the chunk of concrete rubble and smashed his own forehead with it. The blow struck, Mindbender dropped the rock, his eyes rolling back in his head, and lost consciousness. Psy-chick stood behind him, a satisfied smirk adorning her face.

Space Cadet blasted away at Speed Demon's advancing form with the ray gun he'd constructed from the decrepit vehicles lining the city's street. But the superspeedster was too fast.

S.C. fired blast after blast as the human whirlwind closed in on him. Speed Demon sprinted by within inches of S.C. and suddenly the technomancer looked down to find his hands empty and his ray gun missing in action.

Speed Demon raced away and then made a U-turn. Sonic booms echoed behind him, shattering whatever windows remained in the vacant buildings as he increased his speed on his return trip. He rocketed toward Space Cadet, dragging a tornado of vehicles, streetlamps, and garbage cans in his wake.

Space Cadet looked around in desperation. There was no time. No time to make anything. No time to take cover. He was done for.

Speed Demon was mere blocks from Space Cadet when Chance popped out from beneath an open manhole holding Raz's unconscious body in his arms.

"Heythereguyhow'sitgoing?" Chance asked as Speed Demon rocketed past them.

All at once, Speed Demon's powers of superspeed evaporated, negated by his own teammate, Raz. The Invincible and his trailing debris crash-landed, skidded, and rolled along the city street. Speed Demon's unconscious body was the last thing to come to a halt, and it did so at Space Cadet's feet. S.C. placed his foot on Speed Demon's chest. He smiled and raised his arms in victory.

"Yoo-hoo! Mr. Robot!" S.C. called, waving his arms in the air, attempting to gain the attention of a single low-flying skimmer rider. He succeeded and then some. The skimmer wheeled around and shot toward Space Cadet. The Outlaw sprinted for his life down a back alley as the rider chased him with a barrage of laser fire.

Space Cadet vaulted over Private Justice's body, where he lay stretched out flat against the alley floor. As the flying robot dropped low to avoid a catwalk between the two buildings, Private Justice popped up and the robot smacked right into him. As P.J.'s body rebounded, it flung the robot out of the alley and across the street to smack headlong into a building. At that moment, Chance jumped out from behind a Dumpster and snagged the unmanned skimmerboard as it whizzed by him.

He hopped aboard the hovering skimmer and surfed down

the alley, checking the board's equilibrium, getting a feel for its handling. Once Chance was satisfied with his test drive, he turned and addressed his teammates, who had, by this time, gathered in the alley.

"Superion's already inside the volcano, so I've got to get going. I'm counting on you guys to get me through the magma flow at the volcano's top. I have the utmost faith in all of you! Now, let's go win us a championship!"

Chance looked down at Iron Maiden. She slumped against the alley wall, too weak to move. "Don't worry, Maiden. We're going to beat him!"

Iron Maiden nodded.

"Sock it to 'em, Hicksville!" Shocker said as Chance sped upward on his flying skimmer toward the mouth of the volcano.

Once he reached it, he was still able to "see" Gothika concentrating in the lotus position as she hovered a few feet above the city street, thanks to Psy-chick's telepathic link. Psy-chick stood beside her, telepathically relaying the picture of the volcano's mouth, which Chance saw in his mind's eye, to Gothika.

"He's there," Psy-chick said.

"I see it," Gothika said. "I'm trying. But—I'm so weak. It's—hard."

Chance watched as a small section of lava formed a tiny whirlpool. Psy-chick relayed the image to Gothika's mind, helping her to focus her spell where it was needed.

"Come on, Pud!" Shocker said. "Superion's already inside!"

"Almost—" S.C. said, working with feverish speed on a

contraption that was part engine block, part computer circuit board. "There! Done! Give her the juice, Shocker!"

Shocker complied, discharging bolts of electricity from his hands into the machine. Given a power source, the machine sprang to life and emitted a blue glow that enveloped Gothika, serving the purpose for which it was created—the amplification of her powers.

Beneath Chance, the magma pool whirled violently and then opened itself upward into a funnel, revealing the metallic outer shell of the fortress lying beneath. Chance withdrew a magnetic Chancearang and side-armed it onto a section of fortress appearing to be a door. The projectile impacted, static electricity surging through it, causing the door to open. Chance did not hesitate. He plunged downward through the funnel's eye and on through the open door.

Chance raced by a section of hull that appeared as though it had been spot-welded in great haste. *Must have been where Superion entered and then closed the wall behind him. He's in here, all right!*

Chance looked back and saw lava surging down the corridor behind him. *Too bad I don't have laser vision to seal my entrance. Oh well. I guess I'll just have to move with a purpose!*

The fortress was a maze of criss-crossing pipes, catwalks, and tunnels. Chance flew onward and entered a vast steel cavern, the lava covering the floor beneath him. In the room's center, two gigantic pillars of iron and circuitry reached from floor and ceiling to create the power circuit. It was a glowing white disc. It hovered between the tips of the pillars, expelling electrical charges down their lengths.

Chance sighed with relief. He'd made it. They were going to win. But what had become of Superion?

Seconds later, his question was answered.

The opposite end of the cavern exploded in a mass of dust and steel shrapnel to reveal Superion.

They locked eyes, staring each other down like Old West gunfighters. Superion grinned as his eyes powered up, glowing crimson. Chance knew his skimmer couldn't beat his opponent's eye beams to the circuit. So he drew an explosive Chancearang from his belt and hurled it at the glowing disc just as twin laser beams leapt from Superion's eyes. At the exact same moment, both struck the power circuit, obliterating it in its entirety.

Sirens wailed through the air as a wall of steel slammed down behind Chance, damming the lava flow just as it was about to enter the cavern. The hovercams following the championship's action projected large displays of holotext, which read,

DRAW. DRAW. DRAW.

"Impossible!" Superion shrieked. He streaked across the cavern and grabbed Chance by the throat, yanking him off his skimmerboard. "Any fool could see that it was my laser vision which destroyed the power circuit!"

Chance gasped for air as he pawed at the Invincible's arm.

"Release him immediately!" Steel Valkyrie commanded.

Superion turned to see holograms of both Steel Valkyrie and Metatron, his angelic battle instructor, materializing in the air behind him. Superion scowled and looked to Metatron's image. Metatron nodded in affirmation and Superion obeyed, releasing his grip around the Outlaw captain's throat. Chance fell on his skimmerboard. He sat there massaging his throat and gasping for breath.

Superion flew over to his TCT instructor's image and spoke. "This cannot be," he said. "Obviously MOTHER has misjudged!"

"There has been no mistake," Steel Valkyrie's hologram answered. "It appears you both simultaneously destroyed the fortress's power circuit. The contest is a draw."

"It's not fair," Superion whined. "I should've won! I should've won! I should've won!"

"No one," Metatron's hologram said, silencing his student's ravings, "has won yet, Superion."

"What do you mean?" Superion asked.

"The TCT Championship cannot be concluded in a draw. In such a case, the archnemesis rule must be invoked."

"Archnemesis rule?" Superion asked.

"When team competition results in a draw," Metatron's image said, "the rival team captains must face off against each other in singles combat. Isn't that correct, Steel Valkyrie?"

Steel Valkyrie's hologram nodded in reluctant agreement.

Superion grinned, his usual smugness returning to his face. He eyed Chance and the Outlaw gulped in disbelief.

"Furthermore," Metatron's image continued, "the rules of TCT competition state the captain of the team with the most battles logged is allowed choice of competition. I believe you know which type of singles combat competition I would recommend you choose here, Superion?"

If it were possible, Superion's arrogant smile stretched even farther across his face. "Last Man Standing!"

"Excellent choice, indeed," Metatron's hologram said. A smug smile appeared on his face.

"Very well," Steel Valkyrie's image said. "Chance, you, however, are allowed to choose the battle terrain. We will adjourn to the locker rooms. In fifteen minutes, you and Superion are to meet back in the Infinity Chamber for the championship bout."

Chance nodded. But the situation was hopeless.

21

Chance exited the locker room and made his way into the Infinity Chamber. Superion was already there, hovering just above the platform on the other side of the Infinity Posts. Chance took his place on the platform.

"It's still not too late to forfeit, Fortune," Superion said. "Of course, I'm looking forward to tearing the flesh from your bones with my bare hands."

For the briefest of moments, Chance felt the mice of self-doubt begin to nibble at his courage. *You can't be serious,* the mice tittered. *You can't hope to compete here. Not against Superion!*

Chance shook himself and squared his jaw.

Back in your holes, dirty old mice! Chance thought. *You're not facing a scared little boy anymore! Back in your holes before I find a cat to gobble you up!*

And back in their holes the mice of self-doubt went.

"MOTHER," Chance said without taking his eyes from Superion's. "Quadrant 777345345."

Superion frowned and crossed his arms as the Infinity Posts began to power up.

Chance withdrew a pair of plugs from his utility belt and placed them in his ears. Purple-white energy leapt between the posts and reality rent itself in two.

It seemed to Chance as though he was in Superion's clutches even before the purple-white haze of the Infinity Posts faded. "I'm really going to enjoy this, Fortune," Superion said, his smile wide, his eyes feral.

"Tag," Chance said.

"What?" Superion asked. "What are you talking—?"

"You're it!"

Chance pressed a button on his belt and an ear-piercing shriek rent the air. Superion went down, screaming in pain. It was the shrill, unbelieving scream of a toddler who'd taken his first fall headlong into a coffee table.

"You mean you forgot to put in your superreinforced earplugs?" Chance said. "Oh my! Those hypersensitive eardrums of yours must be about to burst right now!"

Chance wasted no further time. He knew that first shot was a freebie. He knew Superion's superhuman healing abilities were even now acclimating the Invincible to the sonic weapon's scream. Chance hoped the psychological damage for someone who didn't even know what pain felt like would be far more substantial, though, for it was a psychological game he intended to play.

He extracted a Chancearang from his utility belt and hurled it at the hovercam tracking his action. Chance was sure the viewers back at Burlington Academy and across Megalopolis in general were shouting in anger as their holograms of him disappeared from view. *Sorry, folks, can't have the hovercam giving away my position.*

Chance bolted from the Infinity Posts, losing himself in the vast, dark labyrinth of industrial machinery to which he'd had MOTHER transport them.

Behold, Chance thought, his mind paraphrasing a line from one of his favorite books, *The Halls of Dwarrowdelf.* The thought had occurred to him due to the towers of machinery stretching from floor to ceiling, like the pillars of the fictitious dwarf city.

He slid on his back down a long stretch of spilled oil and grease. He glided along until he came to a massive power grid. There he got to his feet.

Chance smeared the dark substances covering his back over his entire body, disguising the scent of his clothes, skin, and weapons. He then flipped the large lever adorning the power grid's junction box, the effort taking both hands and his right shoulder. Machinery sprang to life throughout the labyrinth, emitting deafening mechanical cries as its pumps pumped and its cogs turned. Chance then keyed the control of his stealth gauntlet and disappeared in a shimmer of air. He was now undetectable by sight, sound, or smell.

Painful static issued from the plugs in Chance's ears as

Superion's cry of fury echoed throughout the labyrinth. This was followed by the distant sound of rending metal. You didn't have to be a genius to figure out Superion had reached his boiling point and was now laying waste to the cavern.

Okay, Chance thought, *you've got him stupid mad. Good, he's not thinking, not planning. But, on second thought, there's nothing so dangerous as someone oblivious to reason. Especially when that someone can rip through steel as though it were tissue paper! Best to keep moving, stay out of his way.*

And so, for the majority of the next two hours, Chance retreated and hid as Superion advanced and searched. The Invincible encountered many surprises the Outlaw captain had planted for him as he progressed. At best, they were minor inconveniences and only succeeded to fuel Superion's fury. The Invincible held to no predictable course, so it was difficult for Chance to anticipate his direction. There were times when Superion's rampage came within mere yards of the Outlaw captain.

As the championship's time limit neared expiration, Chance decided to make for the Infinity Posts. He surmised the posts were probably the safest location. *Superion shouldn't feel the need to come back there until competition's end.*

But even with the stealth gauntlet running, Chance was uncomfortable exposing himself to the open terrain he'd have to cross to reach the posts. It didn't help matters that Superion was now plucking up machines at the open plain's fringe and tossing them back about the field. With the reduction in running machinery, the clanging din was also reduced. It might be possible for Superion to hear Chance's footsteps as he ran to the posts.

But I'll have to chance it, Chance thought. He reached the end of the machinery not far from Superion's position. He glanced at the Invincible, making sure he was still preoccupied with the machinery's destruction. Chance waited until Superion's hands were on a large turbine and then sprinted across the plain for the posts.

Large engines and gyros crashed down around Chance as he ran, bouncing, rolling, and shattering across the plain upon impact. Chance did not waver in his course. *I'm going to make it, I'm going to make—*

Chance was half the distance to the posts when a steel pipe plunked down onto the ground directly in front of him. There was no dodging it, his momentum was far too great. He tripped over the pipe and hit the ground rolling. His heart sank as he both felt and heard the stealth gauntlet smash against the ground. Blue sparks fluttered over his body and he was visible once again. Out in the open. Alone. Defenseless.

Oh no! Maybe he won't notice—!

"Ready or not, here I come!" The Invincible was upon Chance within nanoseconds.

Chance didn't even realize he'd been hit until he was already flying through the air, blood issuing from his nose as the sensation of pain reached his brain.

He smacked the earth, the air leaving his lungs in a violent torrent. Chance brought his hands up to his face, feeling his swelling nose. *Broken.* The red-and-blue comet of

Superion was on him a breath later, lifting him into the air.

"I'd take out your eyes, but I want you to see the mess I'm going to make of you," Superion said. "Creeper and that electric felon of yours—they got off easy compared to what I'm going to do to you!"

Superion pitched Chance up in the air and caught the Outlaw beneath his arms. Chance screamed as several of his ribs cracked beneath the Invincible's iron grip. Superion laughed with glee and tossed Chance like a rag doll out ahead of him. Chance hit the ground and skidded to a halt within twenty yards of the Infinity Posts.

The capsule! Chance remembered, reaching for the piece of Block's hide stowed down the front of his suit. *Got to open the cap—!*

"Oh no," Superion said, yanking the lead capsule from Chance's hand and tossing it miles off in the distance. "No more tricks." He ripped Chance's utility belt from his body. "No more bombs, gadgets, or surprises! Just me and you. Invincible and Outlaw. God and insect!"

Superion grabbed Chance by the front of his bodysuit and lifted him from the ground. "Do yourself a favor, Fortune, and yield."

Chance looked up, his eyes meeting Superion's. Though Chance's face was a blood-caked bruise, the steel in his soul gleamed out through his eyes as strong and untarnished as ever.

"Never!"

Superion backhanded Chance. The Outlaw soared high into the air, sunbursts exploding across his field of vision, then crashed to the ground. When Chance tried to move his right leg, he found nothing but pain.

"Last chance, *Chance!*" Superion hoisted Chance back into the air. "Yield!"

Chance began to laugh.

Furious, Superion tossed the Outlaw through the air. Chance landed in a bloody heap ten yards on the opposite side of the Infinity Posts.

Superion glided through the air toward Chance, his eyes glowing blood red. "I loathe you, Fortune," he said. "Do you know why? Because I don't understand you—I don't understand any of you mortals! You're different. You're weak. Pathetic. Of no consequence. Of no use. I'd be doing the universe a favor to rid it of your kind!"

Chance lay on the ground massaging his right leg, all but defeated. He slid his hand along his thigh. At his hip, he felt several small, round, hard somethings housed in his pocket. *What's this?* Hope began to rekindle within him.

"So tell me which body part you want roasted first, Fortune," Superion said, hovering between the two Infinity Posts.

Chance reached into his hip pocket and took hold of one of the five smooth marbles lying therein.

"I wonder if the nanodocs can repair your face as easily as they did your friend's," Superion said. "What say we find out?"

Chance raised his hand. One of Jacob's lucky marbles rode on his thumb. "*Oh, shut up, Francis!*"

Chance flipped his thumb and the marble went hurtling through space. It struck the green button on the Infinity Posts's control panel and the twin monoliths roared to life in a blinding purple-white flash. Superion screamed in agony as energy bolts blasted him from either side. Finally, Chance dragged himself to the Infinity Posts's control panel and pressed its deactivation button. The light faded and Superion, his body smoking, fell flat on his face, unconscious.

Holograms of fireworks leapt from between the Infinity Posts. A hologram reading,

WINNER, CHANCE FORTUNE, CAPTAIN OF THE OUTLAWS

scribbled itself into the air and encircled the posts.

I did it, Chance thought, having trouble believing it himself. *I actually won.*

Chance smiled with what teeth he had left, leaned back against one of the posts, and allowed unconsciousness to overtake him.

22

"Hey, champ," Psy-chick said. "Ready to get out of here?"

Chance sat up in his clinic hoverbed.

"Yeah," Chance said. "Just let me get dressed."

"I'll wait for you outside," Psy-chick said and left the room.

Chance got out of bed and walked over to the vanity to wash his face. His limp was all but gone, and the cuts and bruises Superion had left on his face were well on their way to disappearing entirely.

Ah, the marvels of sorcery and modern technology, Chance thought, eyeing himself in the mirror. He'd gone from total incapacitation to almost full recovery in mere days, thanks to the mystic healers and nanodoc machines employed by Burlington's clinic.

Chance went to the closet. It opened with a swish of air. A fresh uniform was ready and waiting for him. Chance suited up, realizing it would be for one of the last times until the spring semester.

Chance thought about everything he'd experienced since coming to Burlington. He'd had adventures worthy of Captain Fearless himself, made the best of friends, and won the Academy championship!

It was the greatest time in Chance's life, everything he'd ever hoped for and dreamed of. He wondered what other astonishing marvels the future held in store for him. He was putting on his mask when he heard Psy-chick scream.

Chance bolted into the hallway. Psy-chick was struggling to free herself from the arms of two supernurses: one male, one female. In front of her, the strange blond-headed boy stood unbuttoning his Hawaiian shirt. Beneath its surface Chance saw things press and wriggle against the fabric, like snakes trying to shed their molted skin.

As quick as lightning, he drew two Chancearangs from the utility pouch at his back. He flicked his wrists, snapping the weapons into their extended semicircular shapes, and let them fly from his hands. Both landed on target, striking the supernurses on their foreheads. They released Psy-chick and slumped to the ground. Chance was at her side a breath later, dragging her down the clinic's main corridor away from the boy. The boy watched them retreat, a scowl across his face. He made no attempt at pursuit—or so it seemed.

As Chance and Psy-chick passed one hall doorway after another, their occupants burst out into the hallway and made chase for them. *What the heck is going on here?* Psy-chick thought to Chance. *Everyone's gone crazy!*

I don't know, Psy-chick, Chance thought back, *but I'll bet it has something to do with that boy.*

Chance and Psy-chick bolted out the clinic exit. "MOTHER," Chance called. "Something's wrong! Seal them in! Now!"

"Sorry, Chance," MOTHER said. "You are not authorized to—"

Chance was no computer whiz like Space Cadet, but he knew his way around them well enough. He keyed a series of numbers into the exit's control panel. A massive steel door slammed down in front of the sliding glass doors just as the clinic occupants were about to erupt through the exit. Chance tossed an electromagnetic bolt onto the control panel. It crackled with blue sparks and smoke rose from the fried circuitry.

Loud booms issued from the door's other side as fist-size dents appeared in its surface. "Come on," Chance said. "That won't hold them for long! We've got to find help!"

Chance grabbed Psy-chick by the wrist and they raced toward McFarlane Cafeteria. Chance was relieved to see Shocker standing on the building's rear steps waving to him.

"Shocker," Chance said. "Man, are we glad to see—"

Chance shoved Psy-chick to the ground as he ducked under the bolt of lightning his best friend had hurled at them.

"Shocker! What are you doing, man? It's us!" Chance and Psy-chick rolled, dodging yet another bolt of Shocker's electricity.

"It's no use," Psy-chick said, grimacing as she focused her telekinetic abilities. A moment later Shocker was knocked backward, unconscious, into the staircase by one of her mental winds. "It's got him, whatever it is." There was no time for them to ponder this, however.

Superhuman students and faculty now swarmed Chance and Psy-chick from every direction, all their friends and enemies among them. The two Outlaws punched and kicked, dodged and darted, fighting for their lives at every turn as they made their way toward Kirby Coliseum.

Chance spied the blond boy watching them from the outskirts of the battle. He drew his grappling gun and fired it at him. The cord wrapped itself around the boy's torso. Chance thumbed the gun's retract button and reeled the boy in, kicking and screaming.

Chance gripped the boy around the neck, holding him so that the boy's back was to his belly. He withdrew a laser cutter from his utility belt and shone a beam of its lowest intensity onto the writhing mass housed within the boy's shirt.

The Outlaws' attackers halted in their steps, their expressions blank, their silence deafening. Chance didn't have to be an empath like Psy-chick to feel the waves of collective hate radiating off of them. He'd been right. Whatever was going on here had everything to do with the thing in the boy's shirt.

"Come a step closer and I fry it!" Chance said. "Back off! I mean it!"

The mass of silent superhumans retreated, granting them a ten-foot berth in every direction.

"What is going on here?" Psy-chick asked, her voice desperate. "What is that thing in his shirt?"

The mob spoke as one, its voice an echoing inhuman wail.

It sounded much like an antique vinyl record being played in reverse. Their words seemed to vibrate into the back of Psy-chick's and Chance's skulls. It was evil given voice, and it terrified the two Outlaws.

"*N'gai, n'gha'ghaa, bug-shoggo, y'hah; Yog-Sothoth, Yog-Sothoth,*" they said. "*WE—ARE—LEGION—FOR WE ARE MANY!*"

The coils housed in the boy's shirt squirmed beneath the light of Chance's laser. "What do you want?" Chance asked.

"*HER,*" Legion said without hesitation, the mob's eyes shifting to Psy-chick.

"Well, you can't have her! Or anything else!"

"*Ph-nglui mglw'nafh Cthulhu R'lyeh wgah'nagl fhtagn!*"

"Fat again yourself!" Chance said. "We're getting out of here and you're going to let us or I turn up the heat! *Got me?*"

The crowd stood silent and unmoving. Chance frowned and increased the laser beam's intensity. The somethings in the boy's shirt writhed. A low, guttural moan issued from the mass of superhumans.

Chance nodded to Psy-chick and approached the perimeter of their free zone. The crowd parted, giving them an open path to the field just beyond the coliseum. Psy-chick and Chance eased their way through, the Outlaw captain keeping the boy close to him and the laser honed on the front of his shirt.

They reached the edge of the mob and walked toward the copse of trees rising from the field's center. The crowd also advanced, but kept the ten-foot berth between itself and the Outlaws.

"Pull that branch," Chance said as he, Psy-chick, and the boy reached the tree. "It opens a tunnel beneath campus. I learned about it from studying blueprints of campus."

Psy-chick pulled the branch. The tree and the section of ground beneath it slid up and over to reveal an entrance tunnel.

"Climb down," Chance said. "As deep as you can!"

Once Psy-chick was in the hole, Chance followed, the boy still in his grasp. Just as Chance and his hostage were about to disappear beneath the surface, Chance hoisted the boy up and out of the hole. He ducked down and pressed the emergency close button just inside the vertical tunnel's entrance. The outside light disappeared from view as the cover slammed closed above them.

Chance stuck an electromagnetic disc onto the close button, disabling it in a flash of sparks and smoke. "That surge will spread. It should seal all the entrances!"

The two Outlaws scampered down the tunnel's ladder, deeper and deeper beneath the earth, moving as fast as their hands and feet would take them.

They reached the bottom and Psy-chick gasped as she looked out and saw the maze of machinery Chance had blundered into months earlier when trying to find Dr. Claremont's class. Chance caught Psy-chick's perception of the mechanized underground from her mind's eye. He saw it reminded her of a damp, smoky boiler room out of a horrorvid where some knife-wielding psychopath stalks and kills teenagers, but enlarged and darkened a hundredfold.

"Come on," Chance said. "We've got to hide! I think we'll

be all right now. I don't think they'll be able to get inside, but I'm not taking any chances!"

Above ground, through the bodies of countless strong-men, blasters, and mystics, Legion pounded away at the sealed tunnel entrance with fists, lasers, and spells. Despite its best efforts, the entrance to the tunnel remained closed and unscathed.

After a time, the battering superhumans halted their efforts in unison, following an unspoken order issued from the intelligence controlling them. Then the mass stepped back, leaving the blond-headed boy standing alone. He looked up into the sky to watch as Alpha-Man floated down through the air to stand beside him.

They gazed at each other, their expressions equally blank. Then the boy opened his shirt. The black slithering tentacles housed therein stretched out toward Alpha-Man, taking the chairman into their grasp. Alpha-Man, already long ago seeded with Legion, accepted the tendrils's embrace without protest.

Legion left the boy, its dark gelatinous mass tunneling into Alpha-Man's every pore. As the creature departed from his body, the boy's eyes rolled back in his head and he collapsed to the ground. Legion's controlling consciousness now possessed a new host—one with the power of a god.

Alpha-Man's eyes grew red with laser light as he turned to peer down at the tunnel entrance. Crimson light shot from his eyes to hammer the steel structure. The metal grew white-hot under the barrage of photons. After some time, a pinhead-size hole opened within the molten slag. Legion forced Alpha-Man's eye beams to increase in intensity and the hole opened even farther, its mouth growing larger and larger.

Chance dragged Psy-chick deeper into the maze, winding down corridors and catwalks of black steel highlighted by the unholy green light of giant electrodes.

Psy-chick screamed in terror as grotesque, ethereal faces came out at them through the walls of dead iron. They snarled, barked, and hissed at the Outlaws, inhuman monsters threatening to tear them to bloody shreds with long claws and scissoring mandibles.

"They can't hurt you," Chance said, waving his hand through the closest apparition, dissipating it into swirls of mist. "They're nothing more than shadows." It was obvious to Chance that Psy-chick was less than convinced.

The Outlaws were at the ledge of a large canyon, its walls comprised of giant circuitry, when they heard the sound of steel being ripped in two.

It was Chance's turn to be terrified. He looked back to see Alpha-Man's silhouette float down out of the entrance tunnel. For a moment, his heart leapt. Just like always, Alpa-Man had swooped down just in time to save the day. But then he saw the ominous red light glaring out from beneath the chairman's shadowed brow, and he knew all was lost.

"They're in," Chance said, all hope gone from his voice. "He's theirs."

Chance and Psy-chick faced each other. "I'm—I'm sorry, Psy-chick. I'm all out of ideas. All out of tricks—*all out of luck.*"

Psy-chick managed a smile though tears cascaded down her smooth cheeks.

Chance wished he'd had the time to tell her he wasn't Chance Fortune, superhuman captain of The Outlaws, but just plain old boring human Josh Blevins of Littleton, Tennessee. There was so much he'd never get to tell her.

The form of Alpha-Man floated toward them, but it was Legion who glared down at the Outlaws through his eyes. Chance pushed Psy-chick from him.

"Run!" he said. "I'll hold him off as long as I can."

"No, Chance," Psy-chick said. "We'll face this together." Chance stood undecided for a moment, then nodded. The Outlaw captain still put his body between Psy-chick's and Alpha-Man's as the demigod flew down to join them on the precipice.

Chance drew his billy clubs and took a fighting stance. "All right then, Legion. Do your worst!"

At that moment, Alpha-Man raised his head to look over and beyond the Outlaws. He looked surprised. Chance and Psy-chick turned to see what held Legion's attention. It was The Dark Thing.

Legion peeled Alpha-Man's lips back into a snarl. "*Boogeyman!*"

The Boogeyman threw back his ebony cloak to reveal a large hi-tech cannon strapped across his shoulder and riding along his hip. He flipped a switch on the weapon and white light climbed through various bulbs along the gun toward the end of its muzzle as it powered up. The gun gave off an ever-increasing digital whine as the light advanced down its side.

Alpha-Man's eyes grew large in shock as The Boogeyman pulled the trigger housed on the cannon's pistol-style grip. The gun discharged, a large beam of blinding white light illuminating the machinery for miles around as it raced from its muzzle to strike Alpha-Man's chest.

Legion screamed with a thousand voices as Alpha-Man's body hurtled backward down into the valley of steel and circuitry below. The Boogeyman raced to the canyon's ledge, Chance and Psy-chick at his heels. They peered down to see Alpha-Man's smoking, inert body sprawled on its back several hundred yards below.

The Boogeyman stared at it for several minutes, making sure the ray gun had done its job. Then he turned and made his way back toward the entrance tunnel, Chance and Psy-chick following behind.

"He did it!" Psy-chick said. She and Chance embraced, jumping up and down in their excitement. "It's over! We won!"

"Wow!" Chance said. "Thank goodness you came!"

The Boogeyman walked on ahead of them, silent and brooding.

"How did you get in here?" Chance asked.

"*I'm The Boogeyman,*" the Board Member said. "*That's* how."

"Yeah," Psy-chick said. "But if you'd been one second later—"

The Boogeyman whirled around to peer down at them, and The Outlaws halted in their tracks, stupefied.

"I'm never late," The Boogeyman said. "And I never lose—"

The Boogeyman went flying through the air in one direction, his laser cannon in the other, swatted like a fly by one of Legion's massive appendages.

Chance and Psy-chick wheeled around to face their attacker. Legion—the true Legion—a monstrous, black nightmare, towered above them, almost touching the chamber's ceiling.

The creature had no true face, but in its center was a gigantic mouth filled with row upon row of serrated fangs. Each one moved as though it had a mind of its own. Enormous ectoplasm-covered tentacles stretched out from the main mass, each with its own smaller version of the central mouth at its end. They all screamed and groaned in the same nonsense language the creature had used when speaking through the Burlington students and faculty.

One tentacle swatted Chance, and he tumbled backward. The Outlaw captain disposed of, Legion turned its attention to its true quarry—Psy-chick. She screamed as the abomination closed in on her, the serrated teeth of its tentacle-stemmed mouths gnashing and biting the air as they encircled her.

The gun.

Chance wasn't sure if he'd actually heard someone speaking, or if yet a new voice had been added to those already bouncing around inside his head. He looked to see if anyone else was nearby, but found no one.

The gun, the voice repeated. In contrast to Legion's loud shrill screams, it was small and still, like a sparrow's song inside a cyclone.

Chance looked up to see The Boogeyman's laser cannon lying in the shadows beneath an atmospheric regulator several yards in front of him. Chance prayed he'd be able to reach it in time.

The Outlaw captain jumped to his feet and ran toward the regulator. Once there, he dropped to the ground and stretched out his arm beneath the contraption, reaching in desperation for the ray gun as Psy-chick's screams echoed in his ears. After what seemed like an eternity, he felt his hand close around the cannon's pistol grip.

Chance jumped up from the ground, the ray gun in hand, and ran toward Legion. He flipped on the cannon's power-up button in midstride. The digital whine sounded, growing ever louder as light rose up through the bulbs on the cannon's surface.

Chance screamed at the top of his lungs.

"LEGION!"

The creature did not turn, but the mouth facing Psy-chick was enveloped by the slimy blackness composing its bulk. The mouth reappeared on the side of the monster facing Chance. Legion's tentacles also shrank in upon themselves and resprouted on Chance's side.

Chance hurled the gun into Legion's mouth. The monster swallowed the cannon whole. Later Chance would think he should have said something clever like, *Have a breath mint!* or *Swallow this!* It's what the superheroes he wished to emulate would've done. But in his terrified, adrenaline-ridden state, such corny banter was the furthest thing from the Outlaw's mind.

Legion made for Chance, all of its mouths shrieking in rage.

The beast faltered as the cannon's digital whine became audible from each of its mouths.

"Get down!" Chance yelled to Psy-chick and ducked. The cannon's white light poured out from all of Legion's murderous jaws.

With no way to release its charge, the cannon erupted within its devourer. Legion exploded, its mass disintegrating in an enormous blast of white light. The shock wave expanded throughout the structure and then reverberated back off its walls several times over.

When the explosion subsided, Chance stumbled over to Psy-chick. He slumped to the ground at her side, and they embraced each other. The Boogeyman hobbled over to them, favoring his left side.

Chance and Psy-chick did not acknowledge him. They sat in silence, trying to come down from the terror still racing through their bodies, just happy to be alive.

With Psy-chick acting as a telepathic relayer, Chance felt the students and faculty aboveground return to their senses now that Legion's control over them had been broken.

Epilogue

Chance stood in a hallway of the Burlington clinic looking through a large window at the blond-headed boy. The boy lay unconscious on a hoverbed, a sophisticated breathing apparatus strapped across his face, along with various other remote diodes monitoring his vital signs.

Chance didn't hear The Boogeyman come up beside him, but he wasn't surprised when he turned to find him standing there.

"Coma," The Boogeyman said, his voice somewhat less ominous than usual. "Doubtful he'll ever come out of it. That alien parasite rode inside him far too long. If only I hadn't been so late in discovering Legion's presence!"

"Who is he?" Chance asked.

"Timothy Grayson," The Boogeyman said. "Probably the most powerful negator to be born in the last fifty years. His parents were found dead in Grover's Mill, New Jersey, just yesterday."

"A negator," Chance said, mulling the fact over in his mind.

"That's why we couldn't detect Legion. Once inside the boy, Legion combined his DNA with its own. It would impart a piece of it and Timothy's accompanying negation powers to each of its victims. Not enough to affect the powers of its hosts, but just enough to prevent its detection. Even MOTHER was oblivious to the creature.

"Legion needed a way to infiltrate the force field and remain unnoticed once inside. Enter Mr. Grayson here. What better way than teleporting in on a negator—a living Trojan horse? Whatever Legion was, it was clever."

"But why Burlington?" Chance asked, sadness in his eyes as he looked at Timothy. "What did it hope to gain?"

"The truth is," The Boogeyman said, "we don't know. Perhaps it wanted to possess the superhuman community. With us in its arsenal, the colonization of Earth—*of the entire universe*—would've been a cakewalk.

"At least," The Boogeyman continued, "I hope that was all Legion had planned."

"Isn't that bad enough?" Chance asked in disbelief. "What else could Legion have been doing?"

There was a moment of silence and then The Boogeyman answered. "Acting as a scout, or envoy."

"An envoy?" Chance asked. "For what?"

"For something—" The Boogeyman said, his red eyes narrowing, "—for something *much* worse."

Chills ran the length of Chance's spine as he contemplated this. He clamped a mental lid down on his imagination before it could paralyze him with fear.

He turned his full attention to The Boogeyman. "I saw him arrive my first day on campus. He—he grabbed me—but didn't attack. Even at the end, he was after Psy-chick, but not me. Why didn't it try to take me?"

"Because," The Boogeyman said, turning from the window to face Chance. "Legion was able to sense *you're human*."

Chance gasped.

"Legion didn't consider you a prize, or a threat," The Boogeyman said. "Its gross underestimation of you proved to be its downfall. But I thought you would have figured that out by now, Chance—or should I say *Pip*!"

The Boogeyman reached inside his cloak, withdrew something, and pitched it to Chance. On reflex, Chance snatched it out of the air. He peered down to see his paperback copy of *Great Expectations* in his hands. He'd left it behind in The Boogeyman's office during his first trip to Megalopolis with the Captain.

Chance was devastated. His cover was blown. The Boogeyman knew. Despite everything he'd done, everything he'd accomplished, Chance had come all this way only to have his dreams shattered. He began to die inside. "What—what are you going to do?"

There was a moment of tense silence and then The Boogeyman spoke. "I've been keeping a close eye on you, Josh. So far you haven't screwed up *too* badly."

The Boogeyman hunched over and looked Chance in the eyes. "*Don't disappoint me.*" He turned to leave.

"Wait," Chance said. "Legion—it didn't try to posses you, either. Not that I saw, anyway."

The Boogeyman paused. "No," he said, and though Chance couldn't be sure, by the tone in his voice he'd have sworn the Board Member was smiling beneath his executioner's hood. "It didn't."

Chance watched as The Boogeyman turned and strode away from him down the hallway. A supernurse pushing a tall hovergurney crossed the hall in his wake. When she moved from Chance's line of sight, The Boogeyman was gone.

Second Epilogue

"Man!" Shocker said. "I can't believe it! The championship title revoked due to alien invasion! Unbelievable!"

Chance Fortune and The Outlaws crossed campus for the teleportation chamber, heading home for the holiday break.

"Not to take away from all that we accomplished, *especially Chance*," Psy-chick said, "but it wouldn't have been fair to the rest of the student body to declare us winners. They may or may not have been competing up to their full potential. They were possessed by a malevolent alien presence, after all!"

"Not The Invincibles!" Gothika said. "Not even us Outlaws until Chance had already defeated Superion!"

"At least," Space Cadet said, his smile beaming up at Chance, "Chance was honored for saving the entire school at today's closing ceremony."

"Yeah," Private Justice said. "But we could've had that trophy!"

"You sound like my mother," Iron Maiden, now fully healed, said. "We don't need a trophy to tell us we're winners, P.J."

Shocker turned to Chance.

"Flarn, Fortune! For someone with good luck as a super-power, sometimes yours ain't so hot!"

"Yeah, well," Chance said as he smiled and shrugged his shoulders, "whatta ya gonna do?"

Chance led the others into the teleportation chamber that had brought them to campus on their first day. "Well, guys. I guess this is it until January."

"Teleportation sequence to activate in sixty seconds," MOTHER said.

"Shocker—" Chance said as he and his electric friend bumped fists.

"Keep it real, Hicksville," Shocker said. "See you on the flip side."

"S.C.—" Chance turned and held his fist out. S.C. bypassed it to give Chance a bear hug. Chance grunted, smiled, and then patted his friend's shoulders. Then he turned to Psy-chick.

Psy-chick giggled nervously. "I hate good-byes."

"Eleven, ten, nine . . ." MOTHER counted.

Chance grinned. "Then let's not say them."

Psy-chick smiled and it was all Chance could do not to be bowled over by the feelings it aroused within him.

"Three, two, one," MOTHER said, "activating teleporta-tion sequence."

"Psy-chick, I—" Chance said. But it was too late. The

white light generated by teleportation swallowed him and his Outlaws, eclipsing his words.

When Chance reintegrated, he immediately knew something was wrong. Burlington Academy was several hours ahead of Littleton, and Chance should've reached home early in the afternoon. Yet, when Chance looked out, all his eyes found was the dark of night.

"Chance?"

It was Space Cadet's voice.

"S.C.," Chance said. "What are you—?" He turned and saw that the rest of The Outlaws were there, as well. All were standing around him, each of them sharing his puzzlement. But Chance was not as puzzled as he wished to believe. Even now suspicions were formulating in his mind—suspicions he dared not entertain.

"What the hurl's going on here, Fortune?" Shocker asked. There was a slight tremor of fear in his voice.

Chance heard the sound of insidious groaning above them. *No! No! Don't let us be where I think we are!*

He looked upward, his gaze tracking to the top of the short, rocky cliffs surrounding them. He saw movement along the ridge tops and heard not only groaning, but hissing and titters of menacing laughter.

"Oh no!" Chance paled with horror. "This can't be. This simply can't be!"

"What are you talking about, Chance?" Iron Maiden asked.

Psy-chick took hold of Chance's wrist, trying to wake him from whatever terror had seized him.

"Chance, please," Psy-chick said. "Tell us. Where are we?"

Chance looked up at her, his eyes wide with fear beneath his mask.

"Oh, Psy-chick," Chance said. *"We're in The Shadow Zone!"*

To Be Continued . . .

Acknowledgments

No one writes a book on their own. Thanks are first due to Michael Lander, Sean Hazelnik, Joe Alegre, and Jay Bonansinga.

And special thanks to my angel, Julie Hahn, and my agent, the Literary Lion, Peter Miller, and everyone at PMA.

And for believing in the story and its unknown author, special thanks to Kathleen Doherty and all the good folks at Tor Books.

My unbounded gratitude goes to my editor and mentor, Susan Chang, who guided me out of the wilderness and into the Promised Land!

And I would truly be a sorry sort, indeed, if I did not thank my wife, Lesley Berryhill, for all her hard work in making this book a success. I love you, Lesley.

Words cannot express my appreciation to the countless authors, comic creators, and Imagineers who filled my youth with awe and wonder—foremost among them being my father, David Berryhill, who recorded bedtime stories of the fantastic on tape for me to listen to when he was away.

And, above all, thanks to Fred Newton Jr.—my friend, sounding board, first editor, and all-around real-life superhero—without whom this book definitely would not have been possible.

All the mistakes are mine.

Shane Berryhill lives with his wife, Lesley, in Chattanooga, Tennessee. *The Adventures of Chance Fortune: Chance Fortune and the Outlaws* is his first novel. To learn more about Shane, visit www.chance-fortune.com.